W9-ACY-927

The Woman Who Owned the Shadows
by Paula Gunn Allen

The Way of the Priests/
The Dark Way/
The White Path
by Robert J. Conley

Waterlily
by Ella Cara Deloria

The Jailing of Cecelia Capture
by Janet Campbell Hale

The Surrounded
by D'Arcy McNickle

House Made of Dawn
by N. Scott Momaday

Ceremony
by Leslie Marmon Silko

The Heirs of Columbus
by Gerald Vizenor

Fools Crow
by James Welch

Black Eagle Child:
The Facepaint Narratives
by Ray A. Young Bear

FIRE
KEEPERS

THE JAILING OF CECELIA CAPTURE

THE JAILING OF CECELIA CAPTURE

JANET CAMPBELL HALE

FIRE
KEEPERS

Quality Paperback Book Club
New York

ONE

No watch. Nobody in the holding tank had one, since all their belongings had been taken away as part of the booking procedure. No clock. No window.

Three or maybe four hours had passed since Cecelia Capture Welles's arrest. Or was it really only an hour or so? It was hard to say because she had been very drunk at the time and she was still not quite sober and was grateful that she wasn't. Being a little drunk took the rough edges off reality. Almost always.

There was time enough to have been transported to the Berkeley jail, hands manacled behind her back. Was that necessary? she wondered. Did they believe that it was? The skin around her wrists was red, and her wrists themselves felt as if they had been bruised, but no bruises were apparent. They would probably show up later, she thought, all blue and purple and ugly.

Mugshots had been taken. At least they hadn't asked her to smile for the camera. She had an uncomfortable thought: The photographs will turn out ugly, because I'm drunk and they didn't let me do my makeup or even run a comb through my hair and this lighting is anything but flattering. At least she had had a good salon cut in San Francisco just the day before, or was it the day before that? It seemed almost humorous to her that she cared how she would look in the mugshots.

She was fingerprinted and given a breathalyzer. The machine was not working right, and the policeman who was trying to administer the test was angry and frustrated. He kept accusing her of not cooperating. His partner came in every few minutes and, speaking in soft, kind, intimate tones, told Cecelia she had better watch out. This other one was mean, he would say, and she had better cooperate or they would have to take a blood sample.

Cecelia told them to stop Mutt-and-Jeffing her. (She had learned about that police method in her criminal law class back in her first year of law school.)

They took the blood sample then, without her permission, which they could legally do because she had given her permission to be tested on the breathalyzer but would not cooperate—or so they would say in the police report, would testify to in court if it came to that. Of course it was because the breathalyzer was not working right and they needed the blood sample for evidence.

She was drunk and therefore somewhat anesthetized and also trying to remain detached from all of this, yet she did feel a surge of anger as she watched them stick the syringe into her unwilling flesh. She felt violated. She watched the tube attached to the syringe fill with her life's blood, deep, dark red. Her very blood was taken without her permission.

Except for the grey concrete floor, the holding tank was painted yellow. It contained a sink and a commode. Long, narrow wooden benches ran along two walls. The room was dirty, gritty, littered with gum wrappers, cigarette butts and empty cigarette packages. It looked as if it hadn't been swept out or otherwise cleaned for a week or more and had held many temporary inhabitants in that time. Its shabbiness matched the shabby way Cecelia felt: unbathed, hair uncombed, teeth unbrushed, still wearing the rumpled clothing she had worn since early the morning before. At least, she thought, there were no wine stains on her dress. The cell had a bad smell to it, too. Just, she supposed, body odor.

Cecelia had two cellmates: Velma and Ethel.

Velma was a thin white whore with needle tracks up and down

her arms. Her teeth were very bad, and her overbleached, dry blond hair hung limply about her face. She had a pale, sickly look, the look a vampire might have, Cecelia thought, if there were such creatures as vampires, and who was she to say there weren't.

Then there was Ethel, a black woman in a black velvet jumpsuit that zipped up the front. The seams strained over her fat, beefy body, her great breasts and her almost unbelievably huge, round, jutting derriere. Ethel had a tough, threatening countenance. She sat on one of the benches, glaring. She told Cecelia to bring her a drink of water, which Cecelia did. Ethel did not say thank you. She drank the water, dropped the Styrofoam cup on the floor and leaned back against the wall, closing her eyes.

Velma wore a bright red miniskirt and a white satin tank top. Thin as she was, her upper arms looked flabby. Her limp hair needed a shampoo. Cecelia thought how strange it was that this woman was desired by men, often, and by many men, so very much desired, in fact, that she was able to earn her living the way she did.

Yet—and she did not just realize this now; she had known it for some time and turned it over in her mind, decided it was not valid, and continued to do it anyway—it was through attracting handsome men that she, Cecelia Capture Welles, sought a measure of self-esteem.

It was through her ability to attract men that she found the assurance that she was an attractive and desirable woman. Maybe her husband didn't want her any more, but she could still get men, plenty of men. But then, so could Velma, and they were willing to pay good, hard-earned cash for the privilege of lying down with Velma. Cecelia wondered if a prostitute's customers kissed her first.

"Hey, girl, what you starin' at?" Velma asked in a loud, hostile voice.

"Nothing," Cecelia said. "I'm not staring." She didn't mean to stare at Velma. It was just that the cell was so small, and there were not many places to cast one's eyes.

"The hell! You just sittin' there starin' a hole through me!"

"You bitches keep it down!" Ethel spoke without moving or

5

opening her eyes. Her tone showed that she meant business. In a quieter voice Velma asked Cecelia what she was in for.

"DUI," Cecelia answered. "Driving under the influence."

"Drunk drivin'," Velma said self-righteously, "is worse than peddlin' your ass. Drunk drivin' kills and cripples. Damages property. Fuckin' never hurt nobody."

"Tha's right," Ethel said, eyes still closed, eyelids completely motionless. She didn't say another word, though both Velma and Cecelia waited for her to continue. But she didn't say anything more, just "Tha's right."

"I know," Cecelia said. It was true. She belonged in jail more than Velma did. Velma spoke with a straight tongue.

Fucking never did hurt anyone, except maybe in a roundabout way. Certainly not the way the drunken driver of a big, powerful, fast-moving automobile could hurt.

She remembered how she had driven aimlessly through the streets of Berkeley in the pouring rain, windshield wipers not turned on. It had seemed cozy inside the old Chevy, the heater making it warm and comfortable, the radio turned to KCOW, the Bay Area country music station. The rain on the windows softened and blurred the outside world, which she already viewed through an alcoholic haze, and she had been crying. Yes, she remembered now, tears and rain and alcohol. What a combination. She had almost managed to blot out the world.

Velma, who had been pacing, sat down on the bench, eyes narrowed, and looked at Cecelia, the woman who knew she was a menace to society and belonged behind bars. Velma studied her carefully, taking her in from head to toe. Twenty-seven, she would guess, or twenty-eight or thereabouts; hard to tell. Dark skinned. Not very dark, but dark enough to show she wasn't white. Mexican, more than likely. Orientals and Mexicans, it seemed, held their ages differently than white people.

She wore a conservative light blue knit dress. Joseph Magnin, probably. Dark shoulder-length hair, newly cut. Velma took in the expensive Italian shoes and the wide gold wedding band on the third finger of her left hand. Velma had known she was a married woman, though, even before she spotted that obnoxious ring.

6

There was just something about her that seemed married.

Velma lit a cigarette.

"Well," she said, "and a married woman, too, huh?"

"Yeah."

"Married women are worse than whores," Velma stated flatly. "Damned hypocrites. I personally have no use for them. Never did. Never will."

Cecelia did not respond. She wished she had a cigarette. Oh, God, but she wished she wasn't there. In jail. Almost anything would have been better. Maybe she should have let Roberto take her home. No. Being in jail was better than that would have been. Imagine waking up beside Roberto.

Velma paced around again, picking at the skin on her arms. Cecelia hoped she wasn't going to start going through withdrawal now. She didn't know anything about heroin addicts, how long they had to go without before withdrawal began.

Velma paced, and Cecelia could see the beads of sweat on her forehead and upper lip. She was apparently very agitated, picking at her skin and pacing. Come on, Velma, Cecelia thought, talk mean and bad some more. Say something. Don't get sick. Velma stopped pacing and sat down.

"The only difference between a married woman and a whore," Velma told Cecelia, "is that they fuck just one dude and get paid a lot less. Then they walk around looking down their noses and thinking they're so good."

Cecelia shrugged, relieved that Velma seemed all right again, at least for the time being. Velma took out her pack of cigarettes and offered Cecelia one, which she accepted gratefully. She needed it.

"Thanks," she said, inhaling deeply.

"Did you call Hubby yet?" Velma asked in a mocking tone.

Cecelia shook her head. Hubby. Her husband, Nathan, was not there. He was in Spokane, Washington, supposedly waiting for her to finish her law degree and return to him and the two children and the house they were buying on a lot and a half in a peaceful little middle-class neighborhood near Northtown Shopping Center.

7

In reality, though, it was not that way. In reality, she knew, her husband wanted her never to come home. He had not been her husband really for a long, long time. He had become another enemy to struggle against and try to keep herself safe from.

"You gonna call him?"

"No. I'm not going to call him."

"What you think he gonna say when he find out his nice little wife been a bad girl?" Cecelia just shook her head, wondering how come a white woman like Velma talked black.

"Humph. Don't matter," Velma said. "You gonna be otta here anyway in just a few hours on OR."

"Most likely will."

"Humph. Don't even make sense," Velma said. "Some irresponsible bitch like you, goin' around endangerin' citizens' lives gets out on OR while a workin' girl like me has to wait for her old man to bring 'round the bail money."

"Well, Velma, that's the way it is," Cecelia said, more to herself than to Velma. She wished she had a drink. She was very nearly sober now, beginning to feel afraid and panicky. She was certainly in no mood for sobriety to take hold.

"Yeah, a married woman is worse than a whore," Velma said again, more to herself than to Cecelia.

The iron door opened and a policewoman stood at the entrance and read: "Welles, please." That was Cecelia's married name. She stood, hopeful. "Come with me," the policewoman said. Cecelia thought she would be released now; they must hold drunken drivers only a few hours on the first offense. Or maybe they would hold her overnight. That would be all right, she guessed. She worried that something might have gone wrong. But what? A case of mistaken identity? Maybe she was the spitting image of some desperado. Maybe it was worse than that. She tried to push such thoughts away. Maybe they were releasing her now.

She was taken along a corridor and up in an elevator. No, they were not going to release her. Panic. Along the way they passed a clock. Three o'clock. Was that all? How could that be? Down another corridor. Then she was put in a cell. Her own cell. Clean and quiet and empty except for herself. She was all alone now and was supposed to lie down and go to sleep, despite the light, which could not be turned off.

She felt afraid. Her body ached. She wanted to go to sleep. A strange thought entered her mind: Saint Jude. Praying to Saint Jude would be in order now. Her mother had often prayed to Saint Jude because he was the patron saint of the down-and-out, the one who helped a person when the situation seemed hopeless. Her mother could pray to Saint Jude, but she could not.

Cecelia lay down and covered herself with the thin jail blanket and closed her eyes. She prayed, not to Saint Jude, but to some unknown factor, please, for oblivion. Just take it all away from me and let me rest. I need to rest.

The one thin blanket Cecelia was given was not enough to keep out the cold and let her fall into a deep sleep. Instead it was a restless sleep. She shifted her position on the thin plastic-coated, sheetless mattress in a futile attempt to get comfortable.

In her dream, a man with a grotesque lined face the texture of rubber peered through a window at her, grinning, as she lay sleeping. Only she was not sleeping. She was conscious, but could not open her eyes, could not move her body, could not force herself awake in order to escape, could not utter a sound, let alone a scream.

Then it was snowing outside, and the window was covered with ice. The man was gone. The window shattered and fell away in thin little pieces, letting in the snow and the cold wind, and still she could only lie there as if in a deep, deep sleep. She could hear the wind blowing. There was the familiar feel of the snow and the sound of the wind during a blizzard as it swept across the frozen hills and echoed through the forest, and then the sound of the coyote howling.

Idaho. Back home on the reservation in Idaho. She still could not move, and the snow fell on her, covered her long, long straight black hair, which lay spread out around her, covered her eyelids and then her entire face. Soon she would be buried in snow, would die when her blood turned to ice. That would be all right. That was the way she always hoped that she would die, like Moses

Brokentooth back home, when she was a child of four, or maybe five.

Moses Brokentooth was from a nearby Montana reservation, the husband of one of her cousins. Moses was always crazy, they said later, cared more for dying than he did for his wife and seven children. The year before, he had tried to die, had held a small gun to his head and fired but succeeded only in partially paralyzing his face, so that he was unable to speak. Then the next year he went out and got drunk one night.

His friends said they let him off at the road leading to his house. It was snowing but not heavily. The house, all lit up, could be plainly seen from the mailbox, where Moses hollowed out a nest for himself in the snow and lay down and polished off a pint of whiskey. They found the empty flask clutched in his frozen hands.

At the wake Cecelia stared at the corpse lying in its casket. Dead, she thought, like the deer her father hunted and brought home and allowed her to help skin and clean.

"You must always cut the throat right away," he instructed her, "to prevent clotting." She never saw him do it because he always did it right after the shooting, on the spot, and he never took her hunting with him.

She remembered how she liked to scrape the innards from the carcass when it was cold, because it warmed her hands. She remembered the way the innards looked: grey and then startling bright red, yellow and purple, as they lay on the stark white snow with the steam rising in the cold air above them.

That was the only death she knew before Moses Brokentooth, the deer death, and she never wondered about their dying, if they had suffered, if they had been terrified, any more than, as an adult, she would wonder such things about the packaged, bloodless hamburger meat or pork chops she bought at the market.

But she did wonder about Moses' dying. They told her no, he did not suffer. Freezing was not like death by fire or drowning or sickness. He had had alcohol in his blood already, which made him feel warm even in the beginning, though he was not. When his blood began to slow, he felt warmer still. By the time his blood froze and his life ended, he was in a deep, warm sleep. No, they said, Moses Brokentooth did not suffer pain or fear.

He looked odd lying dead in his casket, his skin a sort of bluish color. He, whom she had seen only in Levi's and flannel shirts, dressed in a white shirt all buttoned up to the neck, wearing a carefully knotted tie and new grey suit, his hands folded piously and holding a rosary, as if he ever went to church. Cecelia heard the adults saying to each other in low voices when Moses' wife wasn't near how good it was of the priest to allow his burial in hallowed ground. She didn't know what they meant.

Yes, from then on, a frozen death was what she would always hope for for herself when her time came. There would be no pain, no terror, only the cold perceived as warmth and the gradual slowing of the blood in her veins, a deep, warm sleep until her blood froze still.

In her dream she was covered in snow, and the snow continued to fall, and then all there was was stark white. She no longer struggled, unable to move beneath the snow. She was no longer afraid. She lay still and peaceful, accepting the chill, waiting for the warmth she knew would come.

The hollow echo of footsteps in the hallway, the handling of keys and the loud slam of a heavy iron door woke her from the dream.

She lay on the lower berth of an iron bunk bed in a cold, windowless cell illuminated by a single, dim overhead light encased in steel mesh. The cement floor was plain, cracked grey. The cement walls were painted an ugly institutional green, like the walls of an Indian hospital.

That she was in jail was unmistakable. The Berkeley City Jail, of course; it would have to be. How or why she came to be there she could not recall.

Her last clear memory was of leaving law school in the late afternoon after a halfhearted attempt to read the cases and prepare briefs for the next morning. The memory of the night was not lost, though, she could tell. It would all come back. She was in no hurry to remember the events that led her to this dismal little cell.

Her head pounded and her mouth was dry. She was very thirsty. She wondered if the water from the little sink in the corner was safe to drink. Of course it would be. This was not a foreign country. American jails would have to have sanitation standards. She got up off the bed and walked over to the sink, bent down to the faucet and took a long, cool drink, ran the water over her hands, splashed some onto her face. Coming back to life. She wondered why she bothered.

A matron in a Berkeley City Jail uniform brought breakfast: cornflakes in milk, one slice of more-than-one-day-old plain white bread, black coffee in a tin cup. A tin cup. They really used tin cups in jail.

The police matron was a Hispanic, short but very sturdy-looking. Her countenance was stern. She wore her hair in a short, austere style.

"When will I be released?" Cecelia asked her.

She answered only when she had stepped outside the cell, without looking at Cecelia. "Have you been interviewed yet?"

Cecelia wasn't sure what she meant. By whom would she be interviewed? Probably the OR people or the public defender's office. What for? Maybe to determine eligibility. What was happening here? Why was it all getting so complicated? She knew the policewoman wasn't going to give her any answers.

"No, I haven't been interviewed yet," she said.

"Then they should be coming around to interview you. I don't know how soon after that you would be released. It would depend."

"When will they be coming around?"

"Sometime this morning. They only do interviews in the mornings." She slammed the heavy door closed.

Cecelia ate the cornflakes and drank the bitter, lukewarm coffee. The coffee was full of grounds. Cecelia recalled the day before.

Yesterday was Thursday, January 25, 1980. Her birthday. Cecelia Capture Welles was thirty years old yesterday.

She awoke, all alone, in her seedy little furnished apartment.

Her awakening, as always, was sudden and total. It was too dark to see the face of the electric clock that sat on the cardboard box she used as a bedside table. She reached her hand out from under the covers and picked up the clock, drew it close in front of her eyes: five-fifteen. She didn't know why she always had to wake up so early.

Sleeping was difficult for her. She never got enough of it, it seemed. She was almost always a little tired and sleepy, but she could not get to sleep until very late at night and always woke up abruptly around five o'clock.

Rather than lie in bed, awake and restless, Cecelia got up, even though it was indecently early.

The linoleum-covered floor was cold beneath her bare feet. The apartment was cold. It was always cold, because the building was steam-heated only certain hours of the day (she didn't know which was worse, the cold or the clatter and commotion of the ancient radiator when the heat was working) and because Cecelia always slept with the bedroom window open.

Her father had said a person had to have fresh air during sleep, and he kept his window open at night, if just an inch, even in the coldest part of winter, even during a blizzard, and he enjoyed good health throughout his long life.

The open window was a habit she sometimes wished she could break herself of on cold mornings, especially when, like this morning, she woke up with a mild sore throat. *Black's Law Dictionary* held the window open. The book looked important: big and heavy with dark green binding and dignified gold lettering, a book obviously intended for serious purposes, and here it was, propping open a window.

Cecelia made herself a pot of coffee, strong and black. She poured a cupful, then filled her thermos bottle, which she would later put in her briefcase and take along to law school. She sat at the kitchen table holding the cup in both hands to warm them. She sipped her coffee and looked out the window.

Her apartment was on the eighth floor of a decaying old building. She could see all of Berkeley from both her little kitchen window and the big living-room window, all the treetops and streetlights and telephone poles and the rooftops of all the houses and other buildings. Hers was the tallest building in all of Berkeley. She could see the Bay Bridge and San Francisco Bay and the Golden Gate Bridge, and when it was clear enough, which it was not right now, she could see stately San Francisco rising up out of the water on the other side: San Francisco, a dream city of tall white buildings and sparkling colored lights.

Sometimes, now for example, the city would be completely obscured by dense fog, but even when the air was relatively clear, San Francisco, shimmering within a light mist, seemed otherworldly.

Cecelia liked her apartment; cold and shabby as it was, it was *hers* and no one else's. So it had cockroaches. It also had a magnificent view, and because it was in the corner of the building, it had a wide-openness about it, a certain feeling of freedom: high in the sky and not closed in. And, if nothing else, it had character. From the ancient icebox that stood uselessly in one corner of the kitchen to the obsolete gas fixtures and the never-warm-enough, slightly rust-tinted water she drew for her bath each evening, the apartment had character.

The roaches didn't matter to her, or they did matter, but not much, and the rest mattered not at all. The threadbare carpet in the living room, the worn paisley-print linoleum on the floors of the other rooms, the streaked, yellowed wallpaper, the furniture that looked as if it belonged in the lobby of a downtown transient hotel, all of it was just fine. This apartment was part of her now, for all its temporary air.

She had certainly made no effort to "make a home" of this place. On the wall in the kitchen was a calendar she got in the mail from some insurance company and a crayon drawing her daughter, Nicole, had sent her, of a muscleman flexing his biceps and smiling. On the bedside table, which was really a cardboard box, she had placed a framed, glass-covered photo of Corey and Nicole at the ages of twelve and six. Both were smiling and all dressed up in their best clothes for the portrait, their hair neatly combed. Nicole was apparently sitting on Corey's lap. Sometimes

Cecelia spaced-out staring at this photo of her children, and she would wonder if she would ever see them again.

She kept her apartment in appalling condition, with law books and news magazines strewn about and discarded articles of clothing draped here and there over arms of chairs or the back of the couch, and stacks of empty aluminum cans that had once contained diet soda, which she drank while looking out the window or watching TV or studying. Nathan would be horrified if he could see her apartment, the squalor of her surroundings matching the squalor of her soul. She laughed to herself. Even he wouldn't say that: "The squalor of your surroundings matches the squalor of your soul." Yes, he would. He would say anything as long as he thought it might hurt her. When his mother had said, "Imagine, going back to school at your age, Cecelia. I've got to admire you," Nathan had said to her when she expressed hurt and anger, "Well, thirty *is* old to be a law student. You don't think that it is?" She hadn't even been thirty then, but she was now. He would say anything. He was mean and hateful, and she deserved and needed a better husband. So why had one not shown up? Nathan's worthy replacement. That was the way it was supposed to happen. That was what happened in movies once the heroine got away from the bad husband. Here *she* was. Now, where was the male lead?

Cecelia showered quickly in lukewarm water and dressed in what she considered one of her most elegant outfits: an understated light blue knit suit-dress and black suede high-heeled pumps. This is what she would do for herself, she decided: dress up especially well, then take herself out to dinner, to a nice dinner, not to Denney's or Sambo's but to somewhere really nice. She didn't expect that Nathan would call or send a card or letter, but it still hurt her that he wouldn't.

Cecelia applied her makeup looking in the medicine-cabinet mirror, careful not to overdo. She checked her appearance in the full-length mirror on the bathroom door. She hated looking in mirrors. She wanted to look elegant and beautiful, but this mirror couldn't tell her whether or not she did. This stupid, cheap mirror that elongated and distorted one's image could really only tell her the color of her dress and eyes and the length of her hair, and it could, most clearly, tell her that she weighed ten pounds more than she did just one year ago.

How she hated it that she had gained this weight. Ten pounds. Only ten pounds. It didn't sound like much. She stood sideways and held her stomach in, ran her hand across her now flat abdomen, flat as long as she held her breath. It might as well have been fifty pounds, the way it made her feel, all bulgy and bloated and puffy. She sometimes even imagined, as she walked down the street, that she must waddle now. She wanted to throw something at the mirror and break its smug, judgmental, shiny surface. Then the *Berkeley Gazette* headlines would read: FAT WOMAN, OVER THIRTY, TRIES TO LOOK GLAMOROUS AND ELEGANT, RUNS AMOK AND BREAKS OWN MIRROR IN IMPOTENT RAGE.

Cecelia loaded her brown leather briefcase with casebooks for constitutional law and stapled-together xeroxed material for her seminar on the law and psychiatry (a bizarre class at best). She placed the coffee thermos inside the briefcase and fastened it closed.

She didn't *want* to go to that big, windowless concrete block of a building that morning. She never wanted to go, almost never, but it was something she absolutely had to do, no matter how low she felt, no matter how hung over or depressed. It was true that she was often obsessed with notions of suicide. Sometimes she would picture herself driving over a cliff or into the path of an oncoming semi or getting a gun and blowing her brains out (and maybe this was the most often pictured, this last, with the gun held to her temple, the pulling of the trigger and the mighty explosion that would end the pain). But she never daydreamed about dropping out of law school. She had too much invested in it. After all she had gone through to get to law school, and then, having once dropped out, all the trouble involved in returning, she would never quit.

Cecelia Capture was a down-home reservation girl if ever there was one. She grew up poor, was a high school dropout and an unmarried teenage mother. But after many years of struggle, she had managed to graduate not only from college but from Cal Berkeley with honors and had gained admittance to Boalt Hall, one of the toughest, most prestigious law schools in the country. Moreover, for two and a half years she had held her own in that law school with the sons and daughters of congressmen and judges. Her life was in chaos, her marriage most likely dead if not buried. She always hurt inside and lived each day with fear and anxiety. She longed to see her children, longed to have them with her, yet did not feel able to take care of them. Sometimes she thought she might never be strong and whole enough again to resume her maternal responsibilities. But she was studying law, which was orderly and logical and required discipline, and nothing could make her let go of it. She would finish law school if that was the last thing she ever did, and she would attend graduation exercises *alone* if it came to that. (Nathan had only very grudgingly gone to her college graduation, saying he thought the idea foolish, making a big deal out of a twenty-six-year-old woman's graduation. It wasn't as if she was a kid, after all.) She would wear her doctoral academic robes when they conferred the degree of Juris Doctor upon her, and that was going to make up for a whole lot. Anyway, things would get better in time. They would work themselves out. She would stop hurting and begin to lead a good life. She would get her children back. Maybe she would even be able to revive her marriage. That was what she told herself, over and over again, like a chant: "Things will get better. Things will get better."

Cecelia put on her black velvet blazer and took her keys from the nail she had driven into the wall beside the door for the purpose of holding keys. She picked up her briefcase and was about to go out the door when her eyes fell on the vase of yellow roses on the coffee table.

I should throw them out, she thought, poor old things. One dozen yellow roses. They were small and not completely opened when she got them, semi-buds.

She carried the vase into the kitchen, poured out what little water remained, refilled the vase and set it aside to soak. The stems of the roses were rotting, slimy and malodorous, and the blossoms were dried and brown and shriveled.

Cecelia wrapped the remains of the roses in plastic wrap before sticking them in the garbage sack under the sink. She had to wash her hands when she was finished. She wondered why she had let the flowers go for so long. They must have been there for a month, just sitting there on the coffee table, pretty and fresh and yellow and green at first, fading and decaying more and more each day. She had gone about her business, ignoring them and their condition.

A man had given the roses to Cecelia. She couldn't remember his name. It didn't matter. He was just one of those strange men she had had a good time with. He was tall and slim and good-looking, as they all were. This one was a sort of cowboy type, an affectation, of course, since there were no real cowboys in the San Francisco Bay Area. She had met him at the Townhouse in Emeryville. Hearts on Fire was playing that night, or was it Texas Chainsaw? There was a rumor that Hank Williams Jr. was going to show up, as he was known to do, casual and unannounced, and sing a few numbers with the band, but that was nothing but a rumor. Hank didn't show. The man Cecelia met wore western-style clothes: cowboy boots, tight jeans (albeit designer jeans), cowboy hat and sheepskin jacket.

Cecelia had gotten very drunk. This one was a quiet sort of man. She told him he reminded her of a Wild West outlaw. He seemed pleased. He could have played Coleman Younger, she told him. They danced. She felt good. She brought him home with her at the end of the evening. She had never done that with any of the other men. She preferred to go with them to their places because then she was free to leave whenever she felt the urge, but this time it didn't seem to matter. She was feeling silly and giddy and was having fun.

The man she picked up at the Townhouse was all right, just as the others had been all right. There was nothing really special about him. They went to bed together and had mediocre, adequate, drunken sex. But then, the next morning, she had been unable to rouse him, he slept so soundly. She opened the bedroom windows wide and pulled the covers off his pink, naked body. He just lay there sleeping on his stomach, one knee drawn up, face turned to one side.

Cecelia smoked cigarettes and paced around the cluttered apartment, even cleaned it a little, and worried about how she was going to get him up and out, *if* she was going to be able to get rid of him; she berated herself bitterly for being so foolish as to bring him home with her. When he did wake, though, just before noon, he dressed quickly and, after giving her an alcohol-tainted good-bye kiss, left. And she, very unexpectedly, felt sad and empty.

The man didn't ask for her phone number or if he could see her again. They had had a good time. It felt good to be close to another human being, and the orgasm had provided a brief respite. It took her out of herself and her misery. It offered escape more complete than that offered by alcohol, if more brief.

She had got what she wanted from Coleman Younger, she told herself, and didn't care to see him again. That was the way most men felt about sex, and so could she. Yet still, it hurt her somewhere when he left the way he did, with only a stale kiss and the shallow, spoken wish that she "have a nice day."

Cecelia stood near her window and watched the street below. She saw him when he came out, crossed the street, unlocked his car door and climbed inside. He drove a late-model grey Honda. She still stood watching as the car pulled away from the curb and disappeared down the street. She felt empty and lonely and stupid.

Late that afternoon, a florist's delivery man knocked on her door and gave her one dozen fresh yellow roses, and with them, in a little sealed envelope, a card that had written on it: "For you, in fond memory of last night." She immediately put the roses in water in a vase and set the vase on the coffee table and didn't throw the roses away, even when they dried up and grew rotten, because to her they were a tangible reminder that someone had cared about her. Yellow roses. She wondered if he sent roses to every strange woman he picked up and spent the night with. She wished she could remember his name.

Cecelia opened her briefcase and removed the thermos of coffee, took it to the sink and spilled it out. She rinsed the inside of the bottle. She would fill it instead with wine. It would be all right to do that, she decided, just this once, and it wouldn't mean that she was a drunk. It was her birthday, after all, and she needed to celebrate.

Cabernet sauvignon. An excellent choice, she thought, as she poured the wine into the thermos. Burgundy would be too heavy for daytime drinking by itself, and chablis or chardonnay too plain. Besides, cabernet was all she had in her refrigerator. Happy Birthday, she hummed, Happy Birthday to me.

Her car was very old, dented and ugly, an olive-drab Chevrolet she had picked up in Oregon for two hundred dollars when the Ford died on the way down from Washington. The Chevy overheated and burned gas much too fast and stalled at stop signs sometimes. She hardly ever drove it. Parking near the university, if a space could be found, was prohibitively expensive.

She used to take the bus all the way up to the law school, but then AC Transit went on strike, and she would walk the whole distance. Then the rain began to pour down day after day. After that she hitchhiked up University Avenue to the lower edge of campus and walked through to the law school. There were two things wrong with this. She was afraid of the people who stopped and gave her rides, and she didn't like having to walk through the lower campus. It reminded her of the long-ago past, when she was in college. She was young, pretty and vital then, and life was full of possibilities and worth living. It was really not such a long time ago, just six, seven years. The contrast was painful.

The morning of her thirtieth birthday she was not in a hitchhiking mood. Neither was she in a getting-soaked-to-the-skin mood. Dressed in her most expensive dress and her black suede high-heeled pumps and her black velvet blazer, she took the briefcase containing her law books and a thermos full of wine and drove the ugly old Chevy the three miles to the university and paid five dollars to park six blocks away.

When she arrived, it was still early. She went to the coffee shop to go over some class material. She had just opened one of her books when Raul took the chair on the other side of the table. He smiled and told her good morning, asked how she was. Oh, no, she thought, not him. Not so early in the morning. She wasn't in a Raul mood. She was never in a Raul mood.

Raul was twenty-three years old, tall and good-looking, with wavy black hair and brown smooth skin and teeth so white and even that it was hard to believe they were real. He smiled his dazzling smile, much too aware of those good looks, attempting to measure their effect on her. But his beauty was obnoxious to her now rather than dazzling. She wished that he would leave her alone.

She had had an affair with Raul, and when it was all over, she tried her best to avoid him. His insistence that the two of them "remain friends" repelled her, yet she didn't wish to seem immature.

It was awful, the way he always went out of his way to talk to her, made it a point to be friendly-friendly and subject her to all that painful small talk. She wondered if he actually enjoyed it. Sometimes she wished that he would get run over or be seized with an uncontrollable urge to return to L.A., which he said was not "a one-horse town" like San Francisco.

She smiled at him as best she could and told him good morning. He was wearing his letterman's jacket. He always wore that jacket, and it made him seem even younger than he was. The jacket was maroon and white. She hated it.

"Are you going to Atascadero Monday?" he asked her. No, she told him. The law and psychiatry seminar was going to Atascadero, the State Hospital for the Criminally Insane. It was supposed to be a required field trip, but she didn't care. She wasn't going. They would all come back with tales about the wackos. How could she tell them that she envied the wackos their ability to retreat from this world into the realm of insanity? She had a silly thought: What if they were just telling her that this was a field trip in order to get her there?

Because she couldn't make him go away, she and Raul discussed some of the cases they were reading for the seminar. She wished she had the nerve to tell him to buzz off, but she had to act mature and civilized. Nobody got embarrassed because of sex anymore. That was *really* provincial, wasn't it? Probably nobody in swinging L.A. ever got embarrassed about sex or tried to avoid their former sex "partners." Cecelia hated that term "partner." People were business partners and law partners and partners in crime. Butch Cassidy and the Sundance Kid were partners, and so were Abbott and Costello and Burns and Allen. But *sex partners?* Forget it.

The term had such a cold quality about it. Did Rudolph Valentino ever call his women his "partners"? She doubted it. Partners. Cold. Without passion. Without romance. Sexless, actually.

Damn that Raul and his stupid letterman's jacket and his white, even teeth.

He began talking about The Rules of Evidence. Did she understand the exclusionary rule against hearsay evidence? When could what a person said be testified to on the stand and for what purpose? Did she know? He didn't quite.

He had a simpleminded understanding of hearsay, probably acquired watching Perry Mason reruns. Yes, of course she knew. A person under oath could testify that another said something. The person under oath could not testify to the truth of that statement. Raul looked confused. Raul was not going to be a whiz of a lawyer, she thought, and she wondered, for the hundredth time, how it was that he came to be accepted at Boalt.

She drew him a little diagram on a napkin. He listened and watched her and looked as if he were concentrating and trying to understand. Oh, his eyes were dark and deep. Was it any wonder, really, that she had wanted to sleep with him, given the circumstances of her life?

Last August, when the fall semester began, she had noticed Raul. First of all because she noticed all the nonwhite people; there were so very few of them. Then, of course, she noticed him because of his looks. It was hard not to notice him. And he was friendly toward her. That was all, she told herself, just a nice, friendly young man. She was not fully aware of being attracted to him, and she didn't believe that he would be attracted to her.

She used to watch him sometimes before school, in the hallways or out in front of the building, talking with a group of young men. Twenty-three and, like her, in his last year of law school. He had never been out of school. High school, then college, then law. She could remember being twenty-three. She was not so young then. She had a six-year-old son and a year-old daughter, and had supported herself and her son for years before marrying Nathan.

Raul would wait for her in the mornings—for *her*—and they would have coffee together. He was attentive, and they were always "accidentally" touching, touching hands, touching shoulders. She had a dream that she slept with Raul, and her feelings toward him came fully into her consciousness. She felt like a fool. Young, handsome Raul, she thought, how silly. What a silly idea for an almost-thirty housewife from Spokane to have. But she was lonely. She was hungry for the touch of a man, and there was Raul seeming to act as though he wanted her. She was trying to be a faithful wife, even though she had had that one-night slip in Roseberg, Oregon, on her way down to California.

The one-nighter in Roseberg had happened after the hard day when her car burned and she got lost in the mountains and had to spend two hundred dollars on the green Chevy. She met a man in a bar and spent the night with him and felt vindicated after the fight she had had with Nathan before leaving Spokane. She decided that she wouldn't brood over that night in Roseberg. She would even cherish it secretly, remember it when she was old. But, she resolved, there would be no more men. She would remain faithful throughout her stay in Berkeley.

But then there was Raul. And he was no one-night stand. She would sometimes gaze at her face in the mirror on the door of the medicine cabinet and wonder if she was still attractive, if she was still desirable, if she could still attract a man like Raul, or would her sex life from now on be confined to her marriage, or if she was divorced, would she be able to attract only fat, balding,

23

middle-aged men. She would gaze at her reflection and wonder and be unable to judge herself objectively, but, she would think, she must be attractive or Raul wouldn't be interested, he with his great good looks. It would be easy for him to get a young, pretty woman, wouldn't it?

Cecelia had spent a lot of time with Raul. They studied together. They went out to dinner together. They went to the movies together twice. At last he reached for her one night as they sat under the trees on a bench outside Boalt Hall and kissed her deeply and held her full in his arms.

For weeks they were like that: touching, kissing, like all new lovers, unable to get enough touching of each other. She tried to think of nothing but the moment. Raul didn't make a serious sexual advance, though, and she didn't know why, but she did know, from being around Chicanos when she was growing up, that Latino men didn't like women who were aggressive, who made the first move. She waited for him, whatever his reasons were, and it was exciting, and she began to feel young and beautiful and full of vitality. But he didn't make his move.

They sat in his car, like adolescents, kissing and touching. Making out, they used to call it when she was in high school. The first time, on the bench, it was just a few, tentative, gentle kisses and the thrill of being in his arms. But even then she wished that he wouldn't wear that stupid letterman's jacket.

The second time was after they went to a movie, and they sat in his car in the parking lot of the movie theater. It was raining and the lights were amber and they lingered for more than an hour and their kissing became passionate and the windows completely fogged over and her desire for him was overwhelming.

He whispered to her, like a high school boy, and this seemed like a high school encounter, but she enjoyed it as such; he said he could not get close enough to her in those divided front seats. "Why don't we get in the back?"

It was as if he didn't mean it. She was sure that he did not mean it, in fact, and she didn't know why he even asked. When she said no, he accepted it.

His touch those times, during their sessions of making out, was not only gentle but tender, eloquent, even. She enjoyed being held close, she liked his warmth and strength. It was like high school. He didn't seem to expect more. Making out was apparently not foreplay to him, but an end in itself. She began to wonder what was wrong. Was she not truly attractive to him after all? Was he impotent? What was it? What was the matter?

Finally she invited him to spend the night, because she was tired of waiting for him to make the suggestion, and she wanted so much to be really close to him. She longed for intimacy. Did he want to stay, she asked. Are you sure, he said. I don't want to pressure you or anything. Yes, she said, pressing herself closer in his arms. Yes, she was sure. He wasn't pressuring her.

But his lovemaking was strange, not what she had expected. When they lay down together, there were no more kisses and snuggling and tender touches. He was abrupt, mechanical at first, different from the way he had been with her before. She thought he was holding himself back, hiding something from her. Finally he did let go, and that was when she realized that the other way she knew him was totally apart from this new, sexual way.

Like Spencer Tracy transforming himself from Dr. Jekyll to Mr. Hyde, Raul before her very eyes stepped into his sexual persona. She didn't like it. That was what he had been attempting to control, to keep her from seeing.

She wished that he had been successful in holding it back. This was what sex really was for him, not the other, not the long kisses and tender touches but this harsh, ugly way, and it was not what she wanted.

He kept pushing her knees higher, positioning her for his own convenience. It made her feel vulnerable. It was the same position as the one on the gynecologist's examining table, and she loathed it even then, when it had a medical use, loathed being spread apart that way.

Raul whispered to her, "You feel so good. Do you like that? What do you like? Tell me." His voice sounded strange, rougher, unpleasant. And it wasn't just his voice but the way he spoke, too, with a slight Spanish accent. "Talk to me," he said. She thought he had probably had an accent once and had successfully rid himself of it long ago, only sometimes it came back. He drove himself into her. No eloquence now. Like an animal. She felt sick. She wanted it to be over. He whispered an obscenity in Spanish. She knew that this is what it was—obscenity—by his tone; though she didn't understand the words she could tell he was "talking dirty." She held on to him tightly, clung to him hiding her face in his shoulder.

It would not be over quickly. Raul had great stamina and was able to control himself, to keep himself from coming, something he was no doubt very proud of. It went on and on. She hated it. He lifted his body above hers, keeping only their genitals in contact. She could see him in the dim light from the street. He was watching himself fucking her. He moved slowly, pulling his penis almost all the way out, with just the tip left inside, so that he could see almost the whole length of it, watch as he buried it again inside her and as it emerged, glistening wet in the dim light. She couldn't stand it.

"Stop it. Stop, Raul. I don't like that."

He did stop. She turned away from him, from his bewildered look and pulled the sheet over herself.

"What is it?" She didn't answer him. "What's wrong?" She didn't know how to answer him. She didn't know, quite, what was wrong. Maybe what was wrong was all in her. She was no young, innocent girl, after all, and she was not in love with Raul. She had been the one who had invited him to her bed and what she'd wanted from him, truly, was sex. Not love. Just sex. Yet was sex ever really *just sex*? She didn't know what was wrong, then, but she did know his lovemaking, or whatever it was, his brand of sex, was vulgar to her and made her feel bad when she'd wanted it to make her feel good. She wouldn't try to explain anything to him. She just wanted him to go away and leave her alone.

"It makes me feel self-conscious," she said, which was true but not really an explanation.

"You're the only one," he said, "who ever told me she didn't like that. All the others let me do it. Why don't you like it, huh? What are you uptight about? You shouldn't be self-conscious. Sex is for pleasure. I'm not judging you, so don't be self-conscious,

okay? Hey, you think I don't have a little fat around my middle?"
He didn't. His stomach was perfectly flat, his waist, perfectly slim.
She hated him for his stupid remark, for thinking that he was
being reassuring.

"Look," he said, looking into her eyes in the dim light, touching her face, "it doesn't bother me. Some guys it·might, but not
me."

Because he had already begun, she felt obligated to allow him
to continue until he reached his orgasm, and she hated herself for
feeling obligated. Afterward they lay together in the way that men
and women do after sex, but she did not feel close to him. She
felt hurt and angry and wished he were gone. She wanted to tell
him how much it bothered her that he thought she was ashamed
of her body, when it was his own manner that made her feel so
put off, his own lack of sensitivity. At least that was what it had
been. His words kept coming back to her, and she couldn't turn
them off. "It might bother some guys, but not me." She had
wanted to have sex with him because she was starved for intimacy
—and for something else. She needed to feel that she was a
desirable woman. She didn't know that he was condescending in
his attitude toward her, that he regarded her body as something
to be ashamed of. He had humiliated her, and she could not
forgive him for that.

She raised herself up on one elbow and looked at him. Handsome man. He took her hand and kissed it, held it in both of his
against his chest. "Cecelia, Cecelia, my dear . . ." he began.

He said he was going to "lay all his cards on the table." He
would not lie. He hated hurting women more than anything. He
told her he thought she was a "dear, sweet person" and he cared
for her, truly, but he had no strong feeling for her. He liked her,
nothing more. No love. That was it.

"I'm not going to say," he went on, "that we'll try it for a while
and see how it goes, because I don't see anything here to build
on. You're a married woman, after all, and much older. We have
no future together. Do you agree?"

She nodded. Only, she knew, six years did not make her "much
older."

Odd, she thought, here they were lying naked in bed together in the dim light from the streetlamps. They had just had intercourse. Yet she did not feel that they were any closer than they had been. They were, in fact, farther apart. It had seemed so much more intimate when they sat in his bright blue car in the movie theater parking lot.

He went on to tell her that what he wanted with her was a relationship in which each would benefit in terms of warmth, companionship and—he hesitated a bit before he said the word —sex. But it was important that she not feel "used." He didn't want her to think he just wanted to use her as a sexual instrument.

He told her that he had a woman down in Monterey. She was a young divorcée with a child. Sometimes he went to visit her, and when he did he slept with her. He had no deep feelings for this woman, either, but he was not going to stop seeing her.

"What do you think?" he asked Cecelia.

"Thank you, Raul," she said, "for 'laying all your cards on the table.' I don't think it's in the cards for us, though. I don't want a relationship with you."

He was stunned. "You don't want . . . but why? Didn't I satisfy you? You know it would get better. I could satisfy you more after we've been together awhile. It takes some getting used to. People adjust to one another."

"No, Raul." She moved out of his arms and to the edge of the bed, needing now to cover her nakedness. She reached for her robe and slipped it around her. He just lay there, his face turned toward the street.

Before he left, when he was all dressed and ready to go, he made what sounded like a rehearsed speech about how he didn't think any less of her now that they had been to bed together, and hoped they would always "remain friends." He seemed to accept her decision not to see him anymore, though he was clearly bewildered by it.

At the door, when they were saying good-bye, he drew her into his arms, held her close one last time and whispered in her ear, "Is it the other woman, Cecelia? Does that bother you? I'm sorry

I told you. It wouldn't make any difference as far as you and me go. You know that. I would just be with her a weekend now and then. You would never have to see me with her. I wouldn't put her above you."

She pulled back from him and looked up into his eyes. He didn't understand. He really didn't. He was incapable of understanding. She shook her head, remembering how flattered she had been by his attention, how it had made her feel young and beautiful. She could hardly bear the memory now.

"No, Raul. No way. Forget it."

He turned silently and walked down the hall.

More than two months later, on the day of her thirtieth birthday, as Cecelia and Raul sat and looked at each other across the wide expanse of table at the coffee shop, she thought she could still see a trace of that hurt and bewilderment in his dark, dark eyes. He really did not understand what had gone wrong.

She remembered how it had been before their sexual consummation—how she had loved his kisses and the feel of his arms around her, holding her, his body against hers, how she had loved to run her hands over his shoulders and back, all smooth and muscular, and how she had loved looking into those beautiful dark eyes. Poor Raul. He seemed so self-conscious sitting there trying to act casual, so awkward. At last he got up. She wished he would leave her alone.

"Take it easy, now. See you later."

"Bye."

She wanted to cry as she watched him walk away from her in his stupid letterman's jacket. Self-conscious, yes, as he tried to look casual. He probably imagined she had rejected him because he was not a skilled enough lover, or because his stamina was not enough for her. His shoulders were just a little hunched, his head down. That was not the way he had looked before, when each of them seemed in a constant state of joyful expectation. Poor Raul. Poor her. What a fire it could have been.

Tears stung her eyes, but she managed to blink them back. She opened her briefcase and took from among her notebooks and casebooks her thermos. She unscrewed the top, poured herself a thermos-cap cupful of cabernet and drank it down quickly. The second cup she drank slowly, properly. It was just time for her eight o'clock class.

Cecelia sipped the cabernet throughout the day, reciting brilliantly in con law and in labor law. She felt brilliant. Smart. Together. She didn't stumble or grope for words or ideas once. Usually she hated to recite, and even when she was prepared she would say that she was not, to get out of reciting. That day some of her old energy and enthusiasm for the law returned to her, but even as it did she wondered if it wasn't really just the wine, if the next morning she would feel dull and barely able to muster the ambition to get up out of bed, her usual state.

But this day was a good one. If every day could be like this one, she would be all right. If every day could be this good, if she could feel this strong and free of worry, getting through law school would be simple and she would forget about Nathan and her marriage and she would get her children and take good care of them both all by herself.

Before she left the building she made a stop in the women's washroom. Enclosed in the safety and privacy of a stall she poured the one remaining thermos cup of wine and sipped it. Good wine. She had picked it out herself at a winery tasting-room. Good wine had to be drunk in a certain way, a small amount held in the mouth, savored for a time before it was swallowed. It was a long-standing habit, difficult to break: wine simply could not be drunk quickly.

Graffiti on the walls of the enclosure reflected the usual women-in-law-school mentality: "A woman's place is in the house . . . and in the senate." Not very original. Then there was dialogue concerning the ERA.

There was also the old Prosser limerick. When the foremost authority on torts was teaching at Boalt he wrote that limerick for his students, to help them understand and remember the term *De minimis non curat lex*, "The law does not concern itself with small things."

Invoking *De minimis* was in order when the facts and issues were too petty, too trivial, for a court of law to consider seriously. The limerick on the wall of the bathroom stall went:

> There was a law student
> Named Rex,
> Who had an undersized
> Organ of sex.
> When charged with exposure,
> He replied with composure,
> "*De minimis non curat lex.*"

Cecelia considered the doctrine of *de minimis*. She didn't believe it, quite. The law was infinitely capable of concerning itself with trifles, bringing to jury trial people accused of stealing a pen from Woolworth's, for instance. The law, it seemed, was overly concerned with oppressing the poor and upholding the rights of the rich. And it was not true, either, that justice was blind.

Cecelia had finished her wine and replaced the thermos in the briefcase when she realized that two women just outside the stall were talking about her. She was still and listened.

"Welles, Ms. Welles, you know that woman in con law? She recited today. Didn't trip up."

"I know it. Kind of weird, don't you think? The way she seems so spaced-out all the time."

"Yeah, she does. Vague. Yet she knew those cases backwards and forwards, and all the relevant holdings."

"She's a strange one, all right. Seems like she doesn't know or care what's going on, doesn't want to be bothered. But apparently she does know. Weird."

So, Cecelia thought, vague is how she appeared to others. Not true. If anything, she was overly lucid. And they said "knowing" and "caring" as though the two were the same. They were not. She experienced life too sharply, too intensely. What she needed was to become a little more vague.

As for knowing her cases, of course she did. She knew her cases if she had read them. She didn't even have to write a brief on every one of them anymore, the way she used to, and she no longer had to look words and terms up in *Black's Law Dictionary* very often. In fact, she referred to it so seldom it could now be used mainly to prop open windows. She had forgotten to remove the book from the window that morning, and she hoped it wouldn't rain.

The women who were talking about her left. Yes, the wine did help. It mellowed-out everything.

As she was leaving the building for the day, she saw Raul. He smiled at her, and she smiled back and even waved to him, not because she felt friendly toward him now, but because she felt nothing. She didn't even feel uncomfortable at seeing him.

"Hey," Raul said, "you did good in labor law today, real good."

"Think so? Think that I did well? Did it surprise you?"

"No. I didn't mean it like that."

She laughed. She felt liberated from him now. He had no more power over her, or at least none for the moment.

"Are you sure you don't want a ride to Atascadero?" he asked. She shook her head no and headed on down the steps. She felt good.

This was where her memory began to cloud. She had no clear remembrance of going to her car, but of course she must have, because she was driving it. She felt relaxed and in good spirits, had a nice buzz. She could remember that.

Then she was at . . . where was she? Kipp's? The Red Lion? No, it was below street level and there was sawdust on the floor and the noise of electronic games in the background. The place featured live entertainment.

It was either Larry Blake's or . . . Dante's. Yes, that's where she was, she could remember now, Dante's, with the quaint, predictable motto painted on a rough board and nailed above the door: ABANDON ALL HOPE, YE WHO ENTER HERE.

A woman was singing. She was trying to sound like Joan Baez. She was singing an old Baez song:

Old Stewball was a racehorse,

And I wish he were mine,
He never drank water,
He always drank wine.

Cecelia was drinking wine, cheap red wine. Cheap wine and
Baez music. Almost as if Cecelia were not thirty years old and this
were not 1980. She was still Cecelia, though, no matter what her
age, and the year, well, this was still Berkeley, too, no matter what
year.

She passed through the first stage of drunkenness, in which the
almost immobilizing weight of anxiety was lifted from her.
(Wanting this always motivated her to take that first drink.) From
that stage she would enter into a warm, smiling, happy, blissful
state where there was nothing at all to worry about. Everything
was of small consequence. Life was for the living. Everything
could just go ahead and be whatever way it was, and it was all right
with her. Nothing mattered, one way or the other.

That stage would pass quickly, and she would drink more and
more in an effort to return to it or make it stay longer, but that
never happened. Instead she proceeded to the next stage of
drunkenness, the one just before the memory blackouts sometimes occurred.

She was still in the feeling-good stage when the man sat down
at her table. He asked if he could sit down first. Then he asked
if he could buy her a drink. To both she nodded. She didn't really
look at him at first.

"¿Cómo estás, señorita? Me llamo Roberto."

What awful Spanish. Halting. Midwest accent. Worse than
her own, even. He thought she was a Mexican. They always
thought that. Especially in California. Even Mexicans in California mistook her for one of them.

"Encantado, Roberto. Me llamo Carmen. ¿Cómo está usted?
¿De donde es usted?"

He was a big, burly man with small eyes and thinning, light-
colored hair. In his forties, probably. A ruddy-faced gringo. She
giggled drunkenly to herself for thinking of him as a gringo and

at him because he could not even follow her poor, simple college Spanish fast enough to understand what she was saying, and here he was trying to speak Spanish to her.

"No soy Mexicana, Roberto, soy India de Los Estados Unidos and do you know what?" He shook his head. "I'm tired of this godawful wine. Why don't you, Roberto, go buy us a pitcher of margaritas?"

The man nodded, got up from his chair, walked over to the bar, where he had to wait for the bartender to finish making someone else's drinks.

Hussy, she scolded herself, just like one of those shameless cantina girls, hustling drinks from men. Not dignified, I'm afraid, not very. She giggled to herself. A bad woman. She was the kind of woman her father would have called a "bad woman, one of those."

She should have let Roberto believe that she was a Mexican. It went with her drinking name, Carmen. Carmen was what she always told men in bars her name was, and twenty-five years her age and waitressing her occupation.

Waitressing required less explanation and was not so incongruous with the heavy drinking. It did seem a bit incongruous, though, for someone in the last lap of preparing to become an officer of the court, the people's advocate, as it were, to be behaving like a cantina girl. She said twenty-five because she wished that she was twenty-five. She would feel more in step then. She wouldn't be what her husband and mother-in-law thought, so old to be a student. She wouldn't have to be so far behind everyone else then, if she were twenty-five.

And Carmen? Because it was a good fake name. Carmen Miranda, and the femme fatale of the opera *Carmen.* Carmen was a good drinking name. She didn't want her own name associated with her barroom activities.

The ruddy-faced gringo Roberto returned with the pitcher. It sure took him long enough, she thought.

"Ah, Roberto, gracias," she said. *"Muy bueno. Que simpático."*

She poured herself a glassful, lifted it in the man's direction. "To us," she said, tipping the glass and swilling the margarita down all in one gulp, without pause. She smiled sweetly at Roberto and poured herself another.

The guy didn't stand a ghost of a chance with her, no way. No matter how simpatico he might be, no matter how much money he was willing to spend on her cause (getting drunk), it was still no go.

He was, in brief, too short, too fat, too old. She was not that hard up. Not yet. While it was true that she sometimes found strange men to help her make it through the night and was, in fact, interested in finding one tonight, since it was her birthday, she didn't have to settle for a man like Roberto.

The men she picked were tall and good-looking, leading-man types. Carmen liked good-looking men, more than Cecelia did. It was as though different actors were cast in the same role: Carmen takes a lover. A pageant enacted over and over again. How many had there been? After the bad luck with that flaky, insensitive Raul she decided she was going to have her physical needs satisfied whenever she wished and not deny herself the comfort of being with men and not risk what happened with Raul happening again. There were . . . was it five? No, six. Yes, there had been six strange men, six one-night stands. She had gone home with four of them and to a motel with one and she brought one home with her, the one who looked like Coleman Younger, the Old West outlaw, and Coleman Younger had sent her one dozen beautiful yellow roses, which she had kept and kept until they were dried and rotten, and had gotten rid of just that morning.

Roberto smiled at her and reached across the table and touched her hand, which she drew away from him, but not in an unfriendly manner. No, Roberto didn't stand a ghost of a chance with her, and the fact that he thought that he did made her wonder about herself again. This game was getting old. All of it, not just Roberto, but drinking and men in bars. It was all getting old and tiresome.

Cecelia could remember feeling suddenly sad, then, as though she had slipped and fallen into a deep well of sadness, from which there was no escape, or only an escape so difficult it was not worth the effort.

She remembered one time, not so long ago, three years or so. Four. She was just starting law school then. It was their fourth wedding anniversary. She and Nathan played barroom pickup. It was her idea. Come on, Nathan, don't be such an old fuddy-duddy. Don't be such a stick-in-the-mud. Come on, let's do it, it'll be fun.

He didn't want to do it. It was silly. And a little sordid, too. Did he really say that? *Sordid.* Nathan could be such a pain. He didn't want to do it, but he did it for her.

They went to a bar in Northbeach. It was an old beatnik-type coffeehouse. Cecelia went in first (this was her idea, too. "Let me go in first, then give me ten minutes").

Nathan glanced at his wristwatch and went across the street into a bookstore to browse. He was acting irritated. As if she was hard to put up with.

Cecelia didn't know why she wanted to do it. It just seemed it would be fun, and then, because he had made such an issue out of it, it seemed important to her, important that they act it out the way she wanted. Everything was always done his way, she thought, and that way was boring and stuffy and predictable.

The barroom was dark. The front window was stained glass, and at the table near that window some men were playing a game of chess. The bartender was playing a jazz record on the stereo. She couldn't tell jazz musicians apart. It was some jazz record, something a little frantic. It didn't seem to belong here in the dimly lit bar with the slowly progressing chess game. A Bach sonata would have been better, she thought.

The bar was very dark and polished and old, and a mirror ran the length of it on the wall behind. Cecelia sat down on a barstool and ordered a glass of chablis. She was pleased by her reflection. The lights were not just dim but soft and rosy, flattering. In no time at all a man took the barstool beside her and struck up a conversation.

The man was tall and lanky, like a young Gary Cooper, an artsy Northbeach type with a mustache and heavy dark hair that grew not as far as his shoulders but past his collar. She noticed that he had very attractive hands, shapely and strong-looking.

If she had stuck around longer, he would probably have told her that he was an aspiring poet or, more likely, an accomplished but unrecognized poet or maybe a struggling painter. He told her his name was Leon.

"Oh, like one of Madame Bovary's lovers," she said.

"Who? Oh, Madame Bovary's lover, that old porno book by what's-his-name?"

She shook her head.

"Well, then, I don't get it, I guess. Who's this Madame Bovary, anyway?" He motioned to the bartender to bring another drink.

"Oh, nobody important," she said, wishing Nathan would hurry up. Leon looked at her blankly, a little stupidly, she thought.

"Cheers," he said, raising his glass in her direction.

"Cheers," she answered, raising hers.

"Are you from around here?" he asked her. Good, she thought, another topic.

"Oh, no. I'm from Idaho."

"Ah, Idaho. I know it well. Mormons and potatoes," he said.

She was relieved to see Nathan walk through the front door and take the barstool next to her on the other side.

"No," she said to Leon, "that's southern Idaho. I'm from way up north, right on the Canadian border, just a few miles from Montana. In fact, you could stand in my front yard, in Idaho, and the mountains straight ahead would be in British Columbia and the mountains just to the east would be Montana."

"Well, why weren't there any potatoes?" Leon asked. She noticed that his frayed collar was a little soiled.

Nathan was doing a good job of acting casual, as if he didn't mind being in a place like this, as if he were just some guy coming into a bar for a drink, not some put-upon, long-suffering man with a crazy wife who forced him to play silly, sordid games.

Cecelia kept glancing toward Nathan, but he wouldn't notice her. "So," Leon was saying, "don't potatoes grow in northern Idaho or do they just not plant them?" Dumb guy in a bar.

Cecelia saw a woman sitting alone at the other end of the bar give Nathan the once-over, and she felt a stab of possessiveness.

Nathan would still not look at Cecelia. The woman at the end of the bar kept giving him the eye. How very blatant, she thought, no subtlety at all. The woman smiled at Nathan, and he smiled back. She wasn't at all good-looking. Overly made-up, and her low-cut dress, like something in a Frederick's of Hollywood ad, was too contrived to be sexy. Maybe she was a hooker. Probably the kind of woman Nathan would have if he didn't have Cecelia. No doubt. Cecelia felt an intense flash of hostility toward both the strange woman and her husband.

Sooner than she had planned she turned away from Leon and began to talk to Nathan, asking him first for the time.

"Isn't your watch working?" he asked her.

"Well, no. Of course it isn't."

He told her the time.

"Thank you."

What had they talked about? She couldn't remember any more. It seemed as if it was Watergate, but wasn't Watergate all over by then? Whatever they talked about, she couldn't help noticing that he was not entirely unskilled at what he was doing. She would have to discipline herself not to question him about his experiences picking up girls.

Nathan asked if he could buy her a drink, and she accepted. He glanced down at his watch, and she knew he was thinking that they had to get this over with quickly in order to make it to the theater on time. This was before her drinking got really bad, before she had a "drinking problem," but it already bothered Nathan. She had hardly drunk anything all that year, though, so it was all right.

The man she had been talking to, Leon, moved on down the line. Finally he began a conversation with the overly made-up floozy at the end of the bar. Probably the floozy wouldn't be able to tell how stupid Leon was, she thought.

If anyone saw Nathan and me sitting here, if anyone noticed us at all, it would look to them as if we had just met, she thought. It was a giddy, exciting feeling to her, to be "putting one over" on everyone, though she knew that no one cared. Those men playing chess near the front window and those watching the game didn't notice anything, or didn't seem to. The bartender must see a lot of pickups. He nonchalantly washed and dried glasses and wiped off the bar and busied himself emptying ashtrays, doing bartender duties. She knew none of them cared, but still she couldn't help feeling good that she was putting something over on them.

She looked at her husband and tried to see him as though she had just this past few minutes laid eyes on him, and she asked herself, would she still find him attractive, and the answer was: probably yes.

He was five eleven, slender but not slight. Reddish blond hair, lots of it, an unruly mop of blond hair, wire-rimmed glasses, tweed sports coat with leather patches at the elbows. Nathan was nice-looking, not handsome, in a very conventional way, a fine-featured, white Anglo-Saxon. She would have found him not terribly exciting at first meeting but nice and well-mannered and interesting. He looked like what he was: a young Ph.D. candidate, soon to be professor of English at a community college in Spokane, Washington. He would know who Madame Bovary was, and he wouldn't ask stupid questions about why they don't grow potatoes in northern Idaho.

Before they had finished their drinks, Nathan, who kept glancing at his watch, said, "Say, would you like to go somewhere else?"

She smiled. "Do you mean, to your place or mine?" she asked.

He looked pained at her coyness. "I mean, why don't we go somewhere and have some dinner? I'm all alone in the city and could use the company. Unless you have other plans."

"Oh, all right," she said, and that was the end of their game. As they left the bar together, she looked back. No one noticed them, not even Leon or the floozy, who were deeply engrossed in each other by this time.

Once they were outside, Nathan acted short with her. They had to hurry, he said, or they would miss the beginning of the first act. It was a long way to the Geary Theater and then they would have to find a parking space.

He was only indulging her, playing this sleazy game at all.

Sleazy, he said. She had a sleazy streak in her, he would say later in one of their many knock-down marital battles. She was just like the heroine in one of her obnoxious country and western songs.

He was right, too, she acknowledged. She was. She often felt like one of the heroines in a country and western song. They had to hurry to make it to the theater in time. The play they saw was *The Ruling Class*. She couldn't remember anything about it, except that it turned out to be about Jack the Ripper.

She remembered that night and the silly, sleazy game now as she and Roberto sat at a table in Dante's Inferno. Like a character in a country and western song, Cecelia mused. But which song? The one that went, "Love Is Where You Find It"? Or maybe, "Where she waits to be anyone's darlin' "? But that wasn't true. Not *anyone's* darlin'. Not some ruddy-faced gringo's, that was for damned sure.

She smiled at the man sitting across the table from her. He smiled back. She raised her glass to her lips. This place was really beginning to get on her nerves. That Joan Baez singer was just too much:

Oh money can't buy back
Your youth when you're old,
Or friends when you're lonely,
Or a love that's grown cold.

Cecelia started crying. She couldn't stop the tears. The burly man took her by the elbow and tried to get her to leave the bar with him.

"Carmen," he urged, "Carmen, c'mon. Let's get out of here."

She told him, much too loudly, to keep his fucking hands off her and leave her alone.

A waitress came running over to the table looking anxious. Was there anything she could do to help? What was the problem? Did she want her to call a taxi?

"I'll be all right," Cecelia told her, wiping the tears off her face. "Just give me a minute. Then I'll go."

She collected herself, rose to leave, then glanced at the man who sat at her table. She hoped it was a cold, wilting glance. She would make a scene if that man tried to follow her. He looked as if he was going to. He pushed his chair back as if he was about to stand, but she looked hard into his eyes. He looked away. He stayed seated in his chair. She turned and walked out of the bar, up the stairs to the street and out into the cold, foggy night.

Then she was driving aimlessly around Berkeley and crying, for what reason she didn't know. She was drunk, and she felt like crying. Tomorrow was Friday. Oh, Christ. Evidence. Evidence was at eight A.M., and she hadn't read her cases and she was in no shape to do so now. She would be unprepared. Again. Evidence was the least demanding class she had, but somehow she was often unprepared, missed a lot. She sure as hell was not going to be in any shape to learn about . . . what . . . cross examination. "The Ten Commandments of Cross Examination" was the material to be covered first thing in the morning. She had no idea what the commandments were. No evidence tomorrow.

She kept looking at her eyes in the interior rear-view mirror and wiping away the smudged, running mascara.

She drove up Strawberry Canyon, turned around at the Botanical Gardens and came back down again. It began to rain, and she didn't turn on the windshield wipers, and not because she simply neglected to. She liked the windows all covered in raindrops. It made her feel cozy inside the beat-up little Chevy.

She wasn't sure where she was. Down Telegraph, down Shattuck, round and round. She began a turn and then there was that damned flashing red light in the mirror. For just a split second she considered stepping on the gas pedal and making a run for it, but of course she didn't.

Then there she was, standing outside the car in the rain, trying to walk a straight line. What a joke, as if she could. Why, even sober she probably wouldn't have been able to. Who would want to walk a straight line, officer, who in their right mind would want to walk a straight line? And then they were testing her ability to stand on one foot and to touch her thumbs to her nose with her head back and her eyes closed, and she was trying to explain to them that she had never been very well-coordinated. And then:

"You have a right to remain silent. Anything you say can and will be used against you in a court of law. You have a right to an attorney," etc., etc. They were reading her her rights according to the Miranda ruling.

What followed was anticlimactic: mugshots and fingerprinting and an undignified search of her person (for what? narcotics? weapons?). They said she was attempting a wrong turn onto a one-way street. But how could that be? She knew all those old Berkeley streets so well.

Then she was in the slammer. First with Velma and Ethel in a holding tank and now in her own cell. She hadn't been released on OR, and it must be ten o'clock or later. OR was for minor offenders with no criminal records who were considered good risks. OR stood for Own Recognizance, so no bail was necessary. She knew that drunk drivers were usually OR'd. She knew they were not usually kept this long.

She wondered what was happening and hoped that the delay was just a matter of bureaucratic inefficiency, but she knew that it probably was not. Whatever was going on, it was beyond her control at this point, and she tried not to think about it.

No clock. No watch. No writing materials. No other person to talk to. Nothing to read. Just herself, all alone, and the stark green walls of the cell.

Two

The Hispanic policewoman's round, heavily made-up face was expressionless as she opened Cecelia Capture Welles's cell door. She stood outside while a female trustee in a blue denim jail dress and black canvas China-doll shoes with holes worn through the toes entered the cell carrying a brown plastic lunch tray and, stooping, set it down on the floor.

The trustee didn't even glance in Cecelia's direction. Cecelia noticed the dry, inky, artificial-black hair held out of the trustee's face with metal clips and the quarter inch of grey regrowth at the center part. She was much, much too old to have black hair, or ungrey hair—well into her fifties. Cecelia wondered why women of that age, and sometimes older, dyed their hair. Did they imagine that it made them look younger? Did they think they fooled anyone? Maybe it was a habit established when they were much younger, when they had first begun to show some grey, and they just kept on with the dyeing, even after it became unseemly. She noticed that the trustee's fingernails on both hands had been bitten down as far as they possibly could be, and she thought what a strange addiction that was and wondered how a person got started on it. It seemed to her that it must be a difficult thing to begin to do.

Cecelia saw that the policewoman wore a man's heavy gold watch.

"What time is it?" she asked in a small voice, not really expecting a response, since both trustee and guard seemed intent on ignoring her, but the policewoman answered, glancing down at the watch on her wrist, still not looking at the prisoner: "Eleven-fifteen." The voice was as expressionless as the face.

And then they were gone, too quickly, slamming the door behind them. A faint scent of gardenia cologne lingered in the air. It must have been the policewoman, Cecelia thought, because prisoners probably aren't allowed to have things like perfume when they are locked up.

She took the hot tin cup of coffee from the tray and sat down on the lower bunk, holding it. She hadn't noticed until then that it was still chilly in her cell. She held the steaming cup in both hands, warming them, and stared at the tray on the floor.

Lunch was some kind of macaroni-and-tomato-sauce concoction, and even though her stomach rumbled in hunger, her appetite was dead. She thought that if they kept her long enough, she would effortlessly lose those bothersome ten pounds, then ten more, and ten more after that, until she was so thin her collar bones would protrude and her cheeks appear sunken. She would acquire a prison pallor and her hair would grow out long again, the way she had worn it as a young girl, and hang down thick and lustrous black and straight as string to her waist. She would dress in a blue denim jail dress and wear China-doll shoes with holes worn through at the toes. She would look very different from her present carefully groomed, manicured self. She wondered how it would feel to look like that, if it would make her feel more authentic.

She sipped the coffee, which, like the breakfast coffee, was very strong and full of grounds. She considered the cup. She had a tin cup at home in Spokane, and it was almost like this one. She had never used that tin cup to drink out of. She had put it up on a shelf and displayed it in her living room because her son, Corey, had given it to her when he got back from one of his visits with his grandparents. That cup had *The Ponderosa* written on it, and it had the smiling faces of the long-dead Hoss and Little Joe and Pa Cartwright. Corey brought her home a souvenir cup every time he went on a vacation trip with the Donahues, his dead father's parents. She had one with a picture of Old Faithful and one depicting the carving of the four presidents' faces on Mount Rushmore, near the Black Hills. She had another that said *Knotts Berry Farm*. The thought of Corey saddened her, she missed him so much, and then she thought of Nathan, how he had always seemed to be only tolerating Corey ever since he first laid eyes on him, when she and Nathan had first become lovers. She hoped Nathan was treating her son all right now, and she began to worry about their futures, hers and Corey's and Nicole's, now that the family was coming apart, and it was all Cecelia's fault, too. She was guilty of being gone from her family when they needed her and of becoming an adulteress and now, finally, a criminal. She was the selfish one, who had gone back to law school, except that Nathan had wanted her to go.

It was his fault, then. It was his fault she had become an adulteress and disgraced herself this way, landing in jail. She hated Nathan. And she wanted so much to be out of here, to be any-where else, just to be free. She looked into the coffee cup. A swirl of grounds was all that was left. She had downed a lot of grounds while she drank the coffee.

A voice broke the dull silence. "Replace that cup," it said. Cecelia looked around the cell, wondering if she had imagined it. The voice, a gruff-sounding middle-aged woman's voice, repeated the order, only much sterner now, almost threatening. "I said replace the cup. Now."

Cecelia spied the disembodied eye looking in at her through the little window in the iron door. It was a mean-looking eye, she thought, as she replaced the cup in the indented circle on the tray next to the red-stained macaroni. Then she looked to the eye for further directions.

"Now step back," the voice said. She took a small step back-ward. "Way back. All the way back!" Cecelia walked backward until her back was flush against the wall. The door opened and the same black-haired trustee in the blue denim prison dress entered the cell and retrieved the tray and carried it outside, all without glancing in Cecelia's direction. Then she was left alone again, with only her fear, imaginings and ruminations for company.

She lay down, but she couldn't rest. She got up and paced back and forth, back and forth, and this made her feel all the more like a caged animal.

She sat down on the edge of the lower bunk and lightly touched her hand to her throat in a soothing motion because her throat ached inside, felt tight and constricted. She wished she had some more hot coffee. That would make it feel better. She slid back, pushing herself over the smooth, sheetless mattress, until she sat in the shadow of the upper bunk, her eyes shielded from the glare of the harsh artificial light. This is probably how some people get their nail-biting habit, she thought, considering her long, oval nails, neat and even and gleaming with clear varnish. They must start biting their nails when there isn't anything else they can do, she thought, no work, no play, nothing to eat, nothing to smoke. Nothing but one's own body. She remembered reading somewhere that sometimes people with certain kinds of mental disorders will actually tear their own skin.

She drew her knees up close to her body, crossed her arms over her knees and rested her head against her arms. Now, all drawn up in as small a package as she could make of herself and hidden in shadows, she felt a bit safer, a bit less exposed. She could rest this way for a time and let her mind drift, trying to steer it away from the recent past and the disgusting present and the mantra-like chant: What are they going to do with me? When will they let me out? What are they going to do with me? When will they let me out? Away from that. Push it away. Drift on out and away. It's all going to turn out fine. Don't think about it. Let it go. Drift and think of something nice, something fine and pretty.

When she was a little girl of four or five, her mother used to be mean to her sometimes, mean and angry, saying things like

"You dirty little thing you! You're nothing. Just a useless thing. That's all you are. No good to yourself or anyone else. Useless as tits on a boar!" And if she tried to get away she would be grabbed and pulled back, maybe hit or maybe switched, maybe even stuck in the closet. She would have to stay there and pretend that she was paying attention. She would get into trouble if she didn't look at her mother when her mother was performing one of those ugly little monologues, but she didn't really look at her mother. She fixed her gaze on a spot on her mother's forehead, and her mother never knew Cecelia was not looking into her eyes.

Cecelia would then let herself float out of her body until she could look down and see her mother and herself and she would think of . . . Carmen Miranda! She loved Carmen Miranda. Carmen Miranda was the most beautiful woman in the whole world. Cecelia imagined that she was really Carmen Miranda's daughter and they loved each other very much, but one day while they were at a carnival midway with cotton candy and a laughing machine and a roller coaster and a merry-go-round and great swarms of people, her hand had somehow slipped out of her mother's hand and she got lost in the crowd and these people, these Captures, took her home, but this was just a temporary arrangement until her real mother found her and took her back.

When her father came home late at night and woke her from a sound sleep with his drunken stumbling about and falling, his drunken, incoherent cussing and mumbling, she would lie in bed and let her mind go, let herself drift . . . and she would think of Carmen Miranda, all pretty and lively and kind, dancing around and being happy. That would make her feel a warm glow inside, and she would go back to sleep with images of Carmen dancing in her mind.

She had Carmen Miranda coloring books and Carmen Miranda paper dolls, and she would draw her own pictures of the star and color them with crayons.

When she was six and had learned to write words a little, she drew a picture of herself and Carmen Miranda embracing and wrote on it: "Mother and Dotter, Reunited" (her father had told her how to spell "reunited"), and she stuck the drawing on the wall above her bed with a piece of Scotch tape.

Just before she abandoned the Carmen Miranda daydream, she stopped imagining Carmen Miranda as her real mother. Instead she would imagine a grown-up version of herself in full Carmen Miranda regalia, bangles and big gold hoop earrings and bare midriff and, most important, a headdress of fruit. In this daydream she was happy and smiling as she sang and danced her way across the stage, the spotlight following her.

When she got older, she daydreamed of becoming a famous runner, a winner of gold medals at the Olympic Games. She could even see the sportswriters' description of her—"The beautiful, raven-haired Indian maiden from Idaho won again today . . ."—and she could hear the roaring of the crowd, her fans, as she was photographed crossing the finish line.

When she was older still, her imaginings became much less elaborate. She simply imagined herself escaping . . . stealing out in the dead of night, carrying a single suitcase and boarding a bus that would take her far, far away from her parents and into a bright new future. In time, after they had left the first reservation and were living on another, in Washington State, the daydream became more specific. The bus she boarded was a Greyhound bus and on its forehead it said *San Francisco*. This last daydream she made come true at last, the summer she was sixteen. She went to California, and she lived there a long time. She had Corey and she went to college and she met Nathan and married him and she had Nicole and she went to law school and then got sick and had to drop out for a time and then Nathan got a job in Spokane and they moved back to the Northwest and she did not like that. It would suit her fine if the Northwest did not even exist anymore. She didn't like remembering what her life there had been like.

One day, shortly after Cecelia had moved to Spokane, one of her mother's great-nieces, Cousin Em, called her on the phone and asked her to meet her at a bar in the Hillyard to have a drink or two and talk about old times, and she, stupidly, had agreed to this.

Em was one of her mostly white cousins her own age; she had

48

bleached blond hair. As they sat at the small table in the Hillyard honky-tonk with their Black Russians, Em said, "I can remember visiting you guys at your place in Idaho."

Her cousin was a nurse's aide, and she was in her white uniform. The day, outside the air-conditioned bar, was very hot. It was worth the awful bar smell to be in out of the heat. The Black Russians were very strong, and both women were a little drunk.

"Hell, yeah, I remember," her cousin said, "once I got lost in the . . . what was it that grew around there, around you guys' place?"

"Wheat."

"Yeah. In the wheat. It grew so tall nobody could see me, and I couldn't see out. I could hear Momma callin'. I was real scared. I was cryin'. I thought I was goin' to be lost forever."

"Yeah. I remember that, too," Cecelia said. She had known where her Cousin Em was, and she, being much taller, could easily have helped find her, but she didn't want to. She stood silently by, watching, as Em cried and Em's mother frantically searched.

Cecelia's mother's people were white and ashamed of having Indian blood and Indian relatives, and they held themselves far above Cecelia's mother and her husband and children. None of them had gone beyond eighth grade, and they moved around from city to city, from Spokane to Seattle to Tacoma and back again, lived in rented houses and apartments and trailers. They worked as orderlies and short-order cooks and unskilled laborers and went on and off welfare. The women were blond or red-headed and brassy. They wore heavy makeup and swore like sailors and married and divorced often.

For a long time this was the way Cecelia believed all white women were—drifters with low-level jobs who smelled of cheap perfume and married and divorced many men.

"Yeah," her blond cousin said in the Hillyard honky-tonk, "it sure was scary bein' lost in the wheat." She pronounced "wheat" as though there were no *h* in it. "It was scary bein' lost in the weat. And I remember you guys were poor. Oh, Lordy, were you all poor."

"No, we weren't."

"Yeah, you were, too. You didn't even have any electric lights, and you had an outhouse. Ugh. I sure hated goin' into the outside toilet. I sure remember yet how it stunk. And you, you little shit, you threw my doll down that toilet, didn't you?"

"No." Cecelia had done that, but there was no way of proving it even at the time it happened, certainly no way now, and she would never admit that she had.

"It wasn't because we were poor, Em. The power lines didn't go out that far in those days. Everyone who lived out in the country had kerosene lamps and outside toilets."

Em went on and on. Cecelia had always hated her, and she was glad that she had thrown her doll down the toilet. She could understand, too, why she had once hit her on the head with a brick, inflicting a wound that required three stitches. It was not justifiable, but understandable.

"Not poor? How can you sit there and say that with a straight face? Why I remember your momma told my momma once that your daddy got drunk and spent his paycheck and you had to pick up beer bottles alongside the road for lunch money and you had holes in the bottoms of your shoes. You had to line them with newspapers. If that ain't poor, I sure don't know what is."

It was no use, Cecelia knew, trying to explain to Em that that had happened only once, the part about the shoes and the picking up bottles. Damn her mother for discussing that with those awful people.

"So don't you sit there and tell me you weren't poor, Cece." She shook her platinum blond head. Her hair was pinned up in a French twist and heavily lacquered. "You were just the poorest of the poor, that's all, and oh, that awful, ugly old house you guys lived in."

"It wasn't an awful old house. My father built that house himself, and he was a master carpenter. That land where you got lost in the wheat belonged to my father, all of it, all four hundred acres surrounding that house!"

"Now, you look here! Don't you go gettin' cranky with me!"

Cecelia stood up. Her head felt light. She left the bar. She wished she had a brick in her purse. If she had, she would have taken it out and thrown it at Em's head. She heard the shrill voice behind her yelling, "Oh, grow up!" Outside the darkened bar, on the street, the sunlight was blinding.

Cecelia had intended never again to live anywhere near the place where she had grown up, anywhere near her mother or her sisters or her mother's people. But Spokane was where Nathan had found a job.

Her mother's people. White trash. She was surprised that the term leapt so readily into her mind. She had once had such disdain for white people that she couldn't stand blond furniture or light-colored dogs and cats, and now she was married to a blond white man.

Several days after the encounter with Em, Cecelia took Corey and Nicole to her home reservation in Idaho. Nathan was busy working on his classes and didn't want to bothered. It was Sunday. She didn't plan on taking them all so far away, a good hundred-mile drive, but she did. She got in the car and began driving and found herself headed in the direction of the reservation, and then there she was, home again.

She took her children first to historic Ford Butte, where her tribe had fought a battle with the U.S. Army and won, though of course they lost the war, as all the Indian nations had. She told her children that her father's father had been a young warrior in that last Indian war, fought the white people here in this very spot where they now stood. Her father's parents had been among the first Indian people ever made to live on a reservation, and they had been among those few who had survived the great smallpox epidemic when the government issued infected U.S. Army blankets to the Indian people.

"They were old when they had my father," she told her children, "and my father was old when I was born. He was fifty-six when I was born, and that is old to be having children. His parents died many years before I was born."

Nicole had busied herself on the butte filling all the pockets in her dress and sweater with rocks. Everywhere they went, it seemed, Nicole collected rocks.

Cecelia sat down on a big rock, and Nicole sat down close to her, and they looked out over the flat plateau below. Corey wandered away. The butte offered a terrific view. You could see miles and miles in all directions.

Nicole, who was about four at the time, resembled her mother, both of them thought, although no one else did. Because Nicole was white-looking, people were startled to learn that they were mother and daughter, but Cecelia said Nicole didn't really look white, except in a "superficial sense." She was very light-complected and had a small, slightly turned-up Anglo-Saxon nose with a light sprinkling of freckles. But her eyes were another matter. Everyone said that Nicole had her mother's eyes, very large and dark, almond-shaped and intense.

"Did your grandfather have braids, Mom, and did he wear eagle feathers in his hair? Was he a real Indian?"

Corey wasn't even listening to them anymore. He stood watching the hang gliders take off and float away. The day was sunny and windy, and the gliders were out by the dozens. Corey wasn't keen on stories, as Nicole was.

"I don't think he wore braids and feathers, Nicole. Or maybe he did at one time, when he was a young guy, but not when he got older. I saw an old photograph of him once, and he had short hair and wore a big black Stetson hat and was dressed just like a white guy of his day, except for the buckskin moccasins and leggings. He was a real Indian Indian, though."

"What was his name?"

"His name was Eagle Capture. He was named that because when he was young he was very, very good at snaring wild eagles for their feathers. My dad's last name was Eagle Capture, too, until he joined the army during World War I, and then he and his brother both changed their names and they became just 'Capture.'"

"How come? Didn't he like Eagle Capture?"

"I guess not, honey."

"I wouldn't change my name."

"I don't think I would either, but who knows what it was like then? We can only imagine."

52

Nicole nodded her head. Cecelia smiled. Nicole seemed so much older than she was, seemed to understand more, seemed to think on an adult level. But how could she? It had to be that she just gave that appearance. Nicole reached out and took her hand, and the two of them sat for a long time holding hands on Ford Butte, thinking of a bygone era.

Later that day, just before the sun went down, Cecelia took the children to see the house where she had lived until she was twelve years old. It was a long ways out in the country, and the road leading from the highway was all grown over with weeds. The house itself still stood, but just barely. It was faded to a dark brown, dusty color, there were no windows, and the floor was rotting away. The children toured it, amazed that their own mother had lived such a primitive life, without electricity or running water. Cecelia felt anxious and was sorry she had brought them there. Nicole picked up a board from the floor and a lizard darted out from under it and ran across the room. Cecelia shuddered and Nicole screamed. "It was just a little lizard," Corey said in a slightly superior tone. "Harmless."

"Did you ride a horse to school, Mom?" Nicole asked, and she answered no, she had ridden a little yellow bus twenty miles each way, and she was glad that that time of her life had ended because it wasn't any fun, none of it. It was a hard and lonely life, and she would not live that way again for anything. They drove the hundred miles back to Spokane in almost total silence. Cecelia was lost in memories of when she was a girl. It was many years ago, and yet to her now it did not seem long. She could see that house so clearly the way it had been in 1962, when she was twelve.

___THREE

It was April of 1962 and though no snow had fallen in six weeks, the spring was cold and dry, and melting, dirtied patches remained on the ground here and there, in ditches and gullies, in the densely forested areas, in the shadows of mountains, where the sun seldom shone.

It was just daybreak now; the sky, dark and overcast, had been threatening rain since the afternoon before. In her room in the small wooden frame house twelve-year-old Cecelia Capture prepared for the day. She was running a race today at the St. Mary's track meet. Two races, actually, the 660 and the Girl's Relay. The Girl's Relay was not that important, but the 660 was. She was representing Lodi Junior High School.

Cecelia stood in front of the dresser mirror and brushed her hair, which was only somewhat long, an inch or two past her shoulders, not the long, long, past-the-waist length she would have liked it to be.

Her mother nagged her about even this length: "Long and straight and stringy. Why don't you get it cut and put in a good perm? You look just like some old witch. You look like Geronimo.

You look like some damned reservation kid" (which her mother knew that she was but did not like to recognize).

Cecelia brushed and brushed her straight black hair, brushed it smooth and shiny as glass.

Am I attractive? Beautiful? Plain? Just okay? It might depend, she thought, on who her audience was and maybe, too, on what she did.

Surely, if she became an ace runner and won gold medals at the Olympic Games, the sportswriters would describe her as "the beautiful, raven-haired Indian maiden who won all the medals Jim Thorpe had won and then some, who, amazingly, broke records set by Jesse Owens even though her legs were not quite so long."

On the other hand, if she went down to southern Idaho and became a potato picker, or if she waited table at the truck stop in Bonner's, probably nobody would be moved to write about or even comment upon her remarkable beauty. Unless it was some truck driver.

Cecelia lined her eyes, shadowed them in Midnight Blue, coated her lashes with mascara. She stepped back to admire her handiwork.

Liz Taylor, eat your heart out, she thought. She looked glamorous, like an ancient Egyptian princess. Her parents would not tolerate lipstick, but she had no trouble getting away with Egyptian-princess eyes. They never seemed to look at her eyes.

Cecelia emerged from her room at a quarter to seven, carrying her school books and a bundle of running clothes.

Will Capture sat drinking the coffee he had made himself. He was going over his notes and the agenda for the open meeting of the tribal council. The meeting would begin in the late morning and go on into the late afternoon. He had gone over these things before. He wanted to do it again, just one more time. He wanted to be thoroughly prepared.

Will Capture was an ex-prizefighter and he worked to keep himself in shape. He looked ten years younger than his age, which was sixty-seven. He was proud of his youthful appearance.

He always got to the meetings early so he could get together with some people beforehand and talk over the issues. His reading glasses kept getting fogged over by the steam from his coffee, and he had to stop and remove his glasses and wipe the steam away with an old once-white handkerchief.

Cecelia tried to slink past her father quietly without being noticed. She had made it to the door before he saw her.

"Hey, you," he called, "get back in here right now." She was so close to freedom she could reach down and grasp the knob of the door. She didn't move. "I have to catch the bus," she said without even turning around. "No time to get back. It's almost seven."

"Get back here, I said." His voice was flat and not very loud. He looked up at her over the tops of his bifocals. "You have to eat some breakfast," he said. "Go cook yourself a couple of eggs."

"Oh, Dad, for Pete's sake. I'm going to miss the school bus, and there's a track meet today," and besides, she didn't say, she was trying to become as thin as a cracker, as thin as a fashion model.

She would have liked to have a figure like her two oldest sisters, who lived on the coast; they were built the way their mother had been as a young woman, short and petite with no bones to be seen, just soft, rounded curves. But Cecelia and Andrea, the third sister, were built differently. They were tall and sturdy and had prominent bones.

Cecelia was already five feet seven inches tall. She would soon reach what would turn out to be her full adult height of five feet nine inches, but at twelve she worried that she might keep on growing taller and taller until she was an incredible seven-foot-tall woman, and no boy would even want to dance with her unless he was a Watusi or something on that order.

Since she had to be tall, she wanted to be thin, like a model, with hollow cheeks and hip bones that protruded and ribs you could count when she wore a clingy bathing suit and just the slightest suggestion of a bosom. Sleek and streamlined like a greyhound, built for speed. Only she already had, young as she was, more than just the suggestion of a bosom.

"You're not getting out of here without eating some breakfast," her father said, "so you might as well relax. I'll drive you to school in the pickup. I'm going to the agency to a meeting today anyway, and to the dump. I think your mom wants me to do some grocery shopping, too. So just put your things down, take off your coat and fix yourself some eggs."

She did as she was told, but not without glaring her resentment. She wondered how he had such command, although he was so easygoing in his manner. He never used a cuss word, except maybe a "damn" now and then, and she had never heard him really raise his voice in anger. It was hard for her to imagine him as the fierce opponent he was supposed to have been back in his prizefighting days.

Cecelia stood at the wood-burning stove and cracked eggs into the frying pan. She discovered she was hungry. Maybe she would even make herself some toast. No, too much trouble. Eggs were enough.

"Dad, do you want some eggs?"

"No, thanks. I already ate. But bring me some coffee, will you?"

She poured his coffee. He looked up and noticed the bright red sweater she was wearing. She hoped that for once he wouldn't say anything. She was back at the stove when he spoke.

"I don't like that red thing you're wearing." She didn't say a word. "No, I sure don't like it. None but a certain kind of woman wears red."

She knew what he meant, the kind of woman he had in mind. He was so out of step it was pathetic. He was born in 1895, after all. Probably no one else in the whole world who was Cecelia's age had to put up with such an old person for a father. "Grandchild" his friends jokingly called her; she didn't think they even knew her real name.

Cecelia was the child of her parents' old age, twelve years younger than her nearest sister. Odder still, she was not the only old-age child, simply the only one who had survived.

Cecelia didn't know then, as a child of twelve, but she would understand later that she must have been Will Capture's last attempt to have a son, a son who would maybe be the athlete he had always thought he had the potential to become but never was, a son who would become the lawyer he had wanted to be but had failed to become.

Probably he could imagine his son in this big court battle and that one, winning land-claim cases and other sorts, and people saying, "Did you read in the paper about the big water-rights case? The attorney was young Capture, you know, old Will's boy." Will would teach his son from the very beginning the importance of academic discipline. Will's son would form his very thoughts in English. Will's son would provide the Indian people with quality legal representation.

In fact, there were two sons. One was stillborn two years before Cecelia's birth. The other, born a year later, had lived just a few minutes. He was undersized, born too early, and he had managed only a few weak cries, had thrashed his little limbs about weakly, and then had died in his father's arms.

Will Capture had no son in his old age to guide toward the ambitions he had once had for himself. He had only Cecelia, and for a few years he treated her almost as if she were the son that he wanted.

He taught her to excel in school. He taught her the importance of academic discipline. He wouldn't allow her to go to the mission school, where he had gone, where her sisters had gone, because it was not academically sound. He helped her with her homework, drilled her over and over again, listened to her read. When she was home sick, she would get ahead of her classmates because of his coaching.

She was the only Indian child in the town school, and she longed to go to mission school with all the other Indian children, but he said no. He said if you were going to compete successfully in a white man's world, you had to learn to play the white man's game. It was not enough that an Indian be *as good as*; an Indian had to be *better than.*

When Cecelia was eight years old, she skipped third grade, and this made her father proud. Years later he was still finding ways of mentioning this to people, of working it into his conversations. His pride in her was what made going to school in Lodi, which she hated, bearable.

This past year, though, he hadn't seemed at all interested in her studies. He still wanted to look at her report card, and he seemed pleased with her grades, but he was no longer intensely interested. He no longer tested her and drilled her and gave her pep talks about school. She didn't know why he had turned away from her this way. She supposed it was because he took less of an interest in almost everything since his drinking had increased.

"No, Cecelia, I sure don't like to see you wearing that getup." He could be so aggravating. "Getup." Did she wear "getups"?

Of course he would notice that red sweater, which was perfectly respectable, but he would not notice the tight jeans and the eyeliner and shadow and the thick coats of mascara that stuck her lashes together in clumps. Lipstick and rouge and anything red he would notice.

"And another thing," he went on, "you know what they used to say in the old days, when I was a boy? They used to say you could always tell Indians because of the color red. When they saw a rig coming or people riding horses in the distance, they would say, 'Just look for the color red, and you'll know if they're white or Indian.'"

You *had* to say that, didn't you, Cecelia thought, scooping her eggs onto her plate and carrying the plate to the table, clutching a fork in one hand. It was fully light now, so she turned off the kerosene lamp, even though her father was still reading and it would have been more considerate to have let it burn. She sat herself across the table from him and began eating her eggs.

Red was always going to be her favorite color when she grew up, she thought vindictively. Her whole wardrobe would consist of nothing but red. Red coats and red dresses and red high-heeled shoes, red jeans and red nylon stockings. Even red underwear.

Like many Indian people of his generation, her father seemed to Cecelia in some curious way ashamed of being Indian, although he would have denied it vehemently. He spoke the native language, hadn't even begun to learn English until he was twelve and went to mission school.

Cecelia could not help wondering how her father had managed to feel patriotic, why he had enlisted when his father had been defeated in the Indian wars and he himself was not even a U.S. citizen at the time. Her father had taught her a little Indian history when she was small. She knew Indians weren't granted citizenship until 1924. But both of the Capture boys made it over to France to fight Germans on behalf of the United States, as did many, many Indian men, *none* of whom was a U.S. citizen.

She finished eating her fried eggs and poured herself some coffee. Her father continued studying his papers.

He was preparing to argue his liberal political views with the tribal council, that "damned bunch of BIA puppets," as he called them. He had been on the tribal council for a while but was impeached because he was caught sneaking outside for a quick shot of whiskey during a meeting.

Drinking was not allowed on the agency grounds. That was a law first established by his father, Eagle Capture, who had served as tribal judge for many years and who believed that alcohol was the single greatest enemy of the Indian people.

"Those damed BIA puppets would drive Jesus Christ to drink," Will had said when they impeached him, but he still headed up committees and went out and argued his views and got people to vote, and he always took an active role in tribal politics.

He was so absorbed now, she knew he would have to be reminded of the time. She took another sip of coffee. Will's coffee was always strong. It made Cecelia feel grown-up to drink her father's coffee.

She looked out the window. It was a dark, dismal day, and the air felt close. She hoped it wouldn't rain until after the track meet, at least until after the 660. It would be a shame to get rained out.

Cecelia was aware of the beauty of the scene, and when she looked out over the countryside from the kitchen window she thought of the things she had so often heard her father say: that this land belonged to him and he belonged to it, and that he would never leave it again, never, no matter what might happen.

She saw the school bus rumble along the highway and pass the Capture mailbox.

"Dad, the bus."

No response. "Dad, Dad." He looked up from his papers. "The school bus just went by." He glanced down at his wristwatch. It was an old, handsome one, given to him by his father when he graduated from Jesuit High School, before he went away to college.

"We still have a few minutes. Why don't you go put on something else."

Cecelia sat still a few minutes, ready to stand her ground, ready for a fight, she told herself, if it came to that. Her inalienable right to wear what she felt like wearing was at issue here. But now she would feel self-conscious wearing it, anyway. She went to her room and changed to a long-sleeved, crisp white cotton blouse. There, she thought, looking in the mirror, I don't look like a floozy anymore, and nobody can tell that I'm an Indian from a mile away. I hope he's satisfied. He's in for a surprise when he sees all the red I'll wear when I grow up.

Her mother was up making more coffee when Cecelia returned to the kitchen. Her father was outside. He had turned on the engine of the pickup to warm it up and was loading the bed with plastic sacks filled with garbage.

Her mother was a light-skinned, green-eyed half-breed who didn't show her Indian blood at all. When she was young, she had had auburn hair, but it was gone completely grey now, and she had worn it in a short, squarely cut style for as long as Cecelia could remember.

Her mother hadn't put in her false teeth yet. She was short and overweight, and had a double chin, a great sagging bosom and thick ankles. She wore a faded flower-print muumuu. People often said that Mary Theresa Capture had been very pretty once, when Will first married her and brought her to the reservation. Her mother's prettiness was hard for Cecelia to imagine. She had never been pretty in Cecelia's memory.

"Missed your bus, I see," Mary Theresa said without looking at her, the chronic frown tightening her face, as Cecelia put on her sweater. The sweater, she decided, would be better than a coat today. It wasn't really that cold anymore.

"But you've got your dad to drive you, don't you? Your very own private chauffeur. Aren't you the lucky one?"

God, Cecelia thought, how can a person be that way so early in the morning? Didn't even need to warm up first; she was a champion nagger.

Will came in the door, leaving the truck with its engine idling in the yard. At six feet he towered over his wife.

"I'm going into town and to take the garbage to the dump," he told her. "I'll be home sometime in the afternoon, say four or five."

She nodded. She took a piece of folded paper from the pocket of her muumuu and handed it to him. Her grocery list.

He unfolded the list, took his bifocals from his shirt pocket and read it. "What's this," he said in mock alarm, "toilet paper? We're not that fancy around her, not as long as we still have the trusty Sears catalogue."

Mary Theresa smiled slightly at his joke and said, "Then pick up a Ward's catalogue. I'm sick and tired of Sears."

He laughed and replaced the bifocals in his pocket along with the grocery list.

Mary Theresa went to the washstand and tried to lift a dipper of water from the bucket to pour into the white enamel basin to wash her face, but even a dipperful was too much for her to manage with her aching, arthritic hands. Will took the dipper and filled the basin.

Mary Theresa's condition hadn't ever before been as bad as it was this year. Though she had often complained of aching hands and shoulders and knees, still she got around well enough. The arthritis hadn't affected her walk before. Now she walked in a slow, stiff manner that showed she was in pain, not always but sometimes, like today. Cecelia remembered that just summer before last her mother had been strong enough to chop wood and to help carry the washtub full of water outside to empty it. Cecelia knew that her mother's condition was worsening. Anyone could see that.

"It would be nice," Mary Theresa said as her husband performed the task of filling the basin, "to have running water, wouldn't it? Then I wouldn't be such a nuisance. Then I could take care of myself."

He said nothing. Before, when she campaigned to move away, Will always made speeches about how he would never leave. This time he said nothing.

The mention of leaving made Cecelia feel uneasy. This was home in a way no other place could ever be. Yet the idea of leaving was an enticing one, too. The hard part about them all leaving together to live somewhere else was that then there would be no going back, no home to return to.

The road from the house to the highway was rough, and the old Ford pickup rattled and rattled and shook its way along. They had a car, too, a two-door Chevy sedan, which Mary Theresa said looked "undignified" for old people to drive because it was a bright banana-yellow. She would have preferred grey or a nice sedate blue. The Chevy sat all by itself in the yard of the Capture place. Mary Theresa had never learned to drive and was therefore effectively stranded when Will was gone.

When Will and Cecelia came to the highway, Cecelia reached to turn on the radio, but her father signaled her to wait by holding up one finger. He said, "Don't even try to run a race without eating. That's no good. All your energy could leave you all of a sudden. Just like that"—he snapped his fingers—"and you wouldn't be able to take another step. Or you might faint. How would you like that, eh? How would you like to fall on your face in front of all those yahoos at the track meet?"

"Not much," Cecelia said, a vision flashing before her of herself lying in her red gym shorts and white T-shirt, passed out, face down in the dust, while everyone else ran past her. It would be, as he said, "no good."

"All right, then," he said, watching for cars before pulling out onto the narrow ribbon of concrete.

Cecelia would have liked to tune in some rock and roll, to hear a little Chuck Berry or maybe Buddy Holly, but she knew that her father had a strong dislike for music of that sort, and she did like country music. She dialed the country station.

Hank Williams was singing about "Pore Ole Kawliga." A country classic. Kawliga was a wooden cigar store Indian who fell in love with the statue of an Indian maid but was unable to take any action, given that he was what he was.

> Poor ol' Kaw-liga,
> He never got a kiss.
> Poor ol' Kaw-liga
> He don't know what he missed.
> Is it any wonder that his face is red?
> Kaw-liga, that poor ol' wooden head.

Will Capture sang the last chorus of the song along with Hank Williams: "Kaw-liga, that poor ol' wooden head."

They passed a mile-long row of skinny foreign-looking trees growing alongside the highway. Will had planted those trees. That was what he told her once when she was a little girl, and she believed him. She imagined her father out there all alone, à la Johnny Appleseed, personally planting each and every one of those trees.

Actually, he had been part of the highway beautification crew, a WPA program, during the Roosevelt administration, and the crew had planted those trees.

She remembered, too, how she used to think that he had built Grand Coulee Dam, because he had worked there. She could remember taking in the awesome sight of the dam, the tons of white water thundering over it, and thinking that her father had built it, probably with a little help from his friends, just as he had built their house and painted it himself.

Once she had thought nothing was beyond his powers. It was while he was working at Grand Coulee, though, staying in a hotel, that he was robbed and beaten. Two young men, he said later, were waiting for him inside his darkened room and jumped him. They took all his money and beat him badly, broke a rib and an arm.

One of Mary Theresa's sisters and her brother-in-law had driven Cecelia and her mother to Okanogan, where Will had been taken to the hospital. They brought him home with them. His arm was in a cast and a sling. His ribs were taped. Cecelia had never felt quite so secure after that. He was the one who was in charge of keeping her safe. Certainly Mary Theresa could not. If *he* could be beaten up and robbed, rendered helpless by a couple of punks, his bones broken, his money taken, what sort of dangers might befall Cecelia? She was just a little girl. She knew then that even her big, strong, tough father was not capable of keeping her safe always.

They passed the fenced-in Indian property leased by Triangle Cattle Company, where cows grazed, alone and in clumps. They entered the densely forested area, where the road twisted and turned, and came to the place where there was sheer cliff on one side. When Cecelia's sister Andrea was a teenager, she had had a bad accident here in the family car. It was a grey Studebaker, and the insurance had lapsed just the week before. Andrea had had a passenger, one of her friends from mission school. They were coming home from an Audie Murphy movie. It had been raining. The car skidded on the slick road and dropped off down the side of the cliff. Andrea's friend was killed, and Andrea herself badly hurt. The car, of course, was demolished. These were dangerous roads, out on the reservation near Lodi.

"You know," Will said, "it might not be so bad at that, moving away. Your mom's getting so crippled up now I hate to leave her alone, and she's got it so hard out here. Always did. Maybe it's time to move. Your mom and I, we're not getting any younger. We have so little time left now, Mary Theresa and I, just a few more years, and then it will all be over for us."

That was true, but she didn't like to hear it, and it seemed to her he had said it too often this past year.

"And you know something else? I think it would be a good thing if we could live nearer the grandchildren."

They drove through the forested area.

Cecelia nodded, though he wasn't paying any attention to her. She nodded because she was thinking that maybe it wouldn't be so bad, moving away from Route 1, Lodi, Idaho. It was an exciting notion, but a frightening one, too.

Mary Theresa had been a grown woman before she even saw this place, and Will had gone to college in Indiana and done basic training in North Carolina and gone to France and then, when he was in the ring, had spent years roaming far and wide across the country. Cecelia had never been anywhere but Lodi, except to visit her married sisters.

When Will spoke again it was more to himself than to her. "We could make it. I know we could. I'm still strong and able. I could get carpentry jobs working for other old people who can't afford to pay union scale, little jobs on the sly. And with army pension and wheat income, hell, we could manage." Sure, but then he would have to leave his ancestors' bones, wouldn't he, and the land that was his, the house he had built with his own hands, for which he need not pay taxes or rent or utility bills. Cecelia was glad of the sound of the twangy country-western guitar in the cab of the little pickup truck.

Just before reaching town, they came to a green meadow surrounded by forest. This land, meadow and timber, also belonged to Will Capture. It was only ten acres, and it produced no income. It had been Eagle Capture's favorite place to go in the old days, to be alone and to think of things. Sometimes, Will said, his father would go there and stay for three or four days at a time. He liked being there. It was easy to think while he was on that land.

A deer dashed seemingly out of nowhere onto the road in front of them and froze, its dumb face gazing at them. Will applied the brakes and came to a sudden jolting stop. A second passed. Then the deer dashed off to safety, disappearing into the forest on the other side of the road.

The sudden stop dislodged a flask of Jack Daniel's whiskey, which now lay on the floor against Cecelia's feet. She reached down and picked it up. Will put out his hand and drove on, his eyes watching the road straight ahead, and she laid the flask in the palm of his hand. He grasped it and stuck it somewhere inside his heavy overcoat.

66

She hoped that it was just part of his emergency stash and not intended for today. She had to turn her thoughts toward school now. No. No school. Just the track meet today. She had to get in a running mood. She had to put herself in a competing frame of mind.

Will let her off in front of the school, barely in time for the bell. She ran up the walk and the five steps of the red brick building. She turned to wave to him from the top of the steps, but he had already pulled away and wasn't looking back.

In the rear of the truck she could see the boxes of garbage and a big stack of books. She hadn't noticed the books before now. Law books. He was going to get rid of his law books, she thought; he was taking them to the dump. Or did he have them with him because he was going to need them at the meeting? No, that couldn't be it. He wouldn't need all of them. Old, out-of-date law books. He had been given those law books by his dad, Eagle Capture, when he went away to college. Eagle Capture had wanted his son to be a lawyer, and he had jumped the gun a little, going out and buying him a set of law books for a going-away-to-college present along with the gold watch, which was the graduating-from-high-school present. But Eagle Capture didn't know. He was just an old Indian. Eagle Capture didn't even speak English, let alone read or write or know anything about schooling, or much about schooling, even if he was a tribal judge. He didn't know how great the distance was between graduating from high school and practicing law.

Will Capture had told his daughter a lot about old Eagle Capture, how much he had admired his father and wanted to please him. He was the one who had brought the white man's system of justice to the tribe. He believed that the key to survival was legal representation. If the Indian people had had adequate legal representation, there would have been no Little Bighorn or Wounded Knee. It wouldn't have been possible for the white-eyes to steal land and murder Indians. Legal representation was the key. Through the orderly system of laws the Indian people could regain much of what they had lost; they could make sure that treaties were kept, that no more land was stolen and that water rights belonged to the rightful owners. Eagle Capture could not read or write. He could understand English, but he almost never spoke it, Will said, probably because he spoke it so poorly and did not want to appear stupid.

Will had told her how once, when he was a schoolboy, he was with Eagle Capture and they found a gate on their property left open by Grady, a white man whom Eagle Capture permitted to use his land to move cattle across.

Eagle Capture asked Will to write a note to Grady, which he dictated: "Mr. Grady, You keep um gate closed. Me no like um like this. Next time me say you no more use um Eagle Capture's gate." Will had known that his father was speaking improper English, but he had not dared to change one word. He wrote down what his father had dictated and attached the note to the gate. Mr. Grady was never again so careless as to leave the gate open.

Years and years ago, Will's becoming a lawyer had been his and his father's dream. His brother, Mike, wouldn't have been able to do it, and that was okay, because Eagle Capture had two sons. Mike learned English and how to read and write well enough to get by, but not well enough to go on to high school, let alone to college to study law. So Eagle Capture sent Will to Spokane to board with a white family and go to Jesuit High School and prepare for college.

At Jesuit High School Will studied hard and played some good football, helping his school to win the state championship.

In those days, Indians didn't go to high school very often, and the idea of one's going to college was practically unheard of. But Will won a football scholarship to Notre Dame, and he was on his way.

When Will first told this story to Cecelia, when she was a little fourth-grade girl, he said that the short time just before he went away to college must have been the very happiest period of his whole life. It looked as if everything was going to work out right, exactly as he had hoped.

But then there was the game in which he hurt his knee. Just

one more game after that, and football was over for him. And he couldn't keep up with those smart white boys at college. He couldn't, no matter how hard he tried. English was not his native language, and he had to stop and translate where they did not. They knew more. Their minds were nimbler than his, and he could not compete. No amount of study helped, and he flunked out. But Cecelia, he told her, was going to be different; she was not even going to learn to speak the native tongue, although all her sisters knew it. Then she would have to look at the world and see it as any English-speaking person does, would be forced to form her thoughts in English, and would be able to keep up with any white person. Work, work, work. Study, study, study. It wasn't enough, he told her, to be okay, to hold her own; she had to do better, much better, if she was going to survive in a white man's world.

Cecelia had heard the story many, many times about her father's wanting to be a lawyer, and how the Indian people had a great, great need for high-quality legal representation, and why it was the duty of any Indian person able to become a lawyer to become one and then dedicate his professional life to helping his people obtain justice. No father could be prouder than her father was of how well she did in school, and once or twice he kidded her in a way that she didn't like, that she wouldn't like even when she was a grown woman and he was dead and she was remembering him. She would think that it was no way for a father to kid a daughter. He would tell her, "It's too bad that you're a girl, Cece, because, you know, men just don't like smart women. When you grow up, you are going to have to pretend to be dumb or else you're never going to get a husband."

The part of her father's life that followed the war was not told to her when she was a young child, but she knew it very well by the time she was twelve. It had caused her a lot of pain. Her mother was the first one to tell her, and her motive was unclear. It probably came up on one of those occasions when her mother was telling her how she was just like her father and would grow up to be just like him, and he was no damned good. The story involved his near-murder of a white man and the subsequent time he had spent in the Colorado State Penitentiary. Her father was an ex-convict.

That story had haunted her from the time her mother first told it to her when she was nine or ten. Then her father told her about it himself. He said he was telling her because it was well known and he was afraid she might hear it from some gossip and it would hurt her, so he wanted her to hear it from him. It made a little more sense when her father told the story, but it was essentially the same. Many years later, when she was twenty-nine and living in Spokane and her father was long dead, a drunk woman from her tribe came up to Cecelia in a bar, where Cecelia was herself attempting to get drunk, and said she knew her father, Will Capture, had known him very well, in fact, and she told the story a third time, beginning, "I remember when that incident in Colorado happened. Everyone was talking about it. When he went to trial, it was written up in the tribal newspaper. It wasn't his fault, the way it happened. Not all of it, the way he told it, anyway, but then nobody really knows who wasn't there . . . but this is how I heard it . . ." And so she had to hear the tale a third time, had to endure it again when she least expected it, from a drunken, foolish source.

The story went like this: After the war was over, Will did not return to Idaho. He didn't feel like going back. Eagle Capture was dead. There was nothing there for him, and he felt restless. He hadn't expected to survive the war—that was why he had been so decorated, because he thought he was going to die, and it didn't matter. It wasn't really that he was so awfully brave. But he did survive, and then he didn't know quite what to do with himself.

He entered the ring professionally, and he roamed the country, prizefighting and boozing. There was a law in effect then, repealed only in 1954, against selling alcoholic beverages to Indians, but those laws were enforced only in dumb little reservation towns. In the places he traveled—Chicago, L.A., San Francisco, New Orleans—nobody knew of such a law, or if they did, they didn't care. Fighting, boozing, barroom brawling, that was the life of the war hero after the war was over.

He was in Denver once, and he was in a tavern, and he was drunk. A white man called him chief. He thought he was being chummy by calling him that. "Chief," he said in a friendly, familiar way. Will Capture didn't like it when white men called him chief. His comrades-in-arms had called him chief, and he hadn't minded it then, at least not at first. He had taken it as a show of respect: a chief, which he certainly was not, was accorded great respect. But he came to understand it as a mockery when they called him that, a mockery of him and of his people and of what it meant to be a chief.

And he would hear it said time and time again, in that humorous, mocking tone, even at times when he was really down and out, penniless because he'd blown all his money on a binge, and was panhandling in the street in his dirty, rumpled clothing. Some benevolent passerby would drop a dime or a quarter into his outstretched, begging palm and say, "Here, chief, get yourself a cup of coffee," and he would fight down the bitter bile taste in his mouth and smile his thanks.

Except that last time with the poor stupid white-eyes in the tavern in Denver, who testified in court that he had only wanted to buy him a beer, that he had no idea the big Indian would get insulted, why, he called all Indians "chief"—didn't everybody? All nigger men were "boy" and all Indian men were "chief." That was the way it was. He didn't mean anything by it.

Only that wasn't all he had said. If he had let it go at that, it might have been all right. That particular white man, though, had a taste for Indian women. Will had heard him tell another man in the bar that he had a taste for squaws, for "dark meat," acquired when he worked for a time in Nevada.

He bought Will Capture a beer, made some "friendly" small talk, addressing him as "chief" all the while. Will was good and drunk by then. He sat there on his barstool with his head down, his body all hunched over.

The white man leaned his face closer to Will and lowered his voice to an intimate level. He said he sure would like to get himself a hot little squaw for the night and could the chief help him find one? There would be a little something in it for him.

The white man, whose name turned out to be Russell, testified in court: "Then, for the first time, he turned and looked into my face."

It was a smiling, leering face Will Capture looked into, and Russell's breath reeked of garlic and beer.

"I hadn't realized, not until that moment, how drunk he really was. He was sitting up straight and looking at me, and his eyes were narrow, evil-looking slits." But Russell didn't move. He sat there, that stupid grin on his face, waiting for a reply to his question about the "hot little squaw" he hoped to find to spend the night with.

"Then," Russell continued, "the first blow landed, breaking my jaw. God, I didn't even see it coming."

What Will Capture would remember about that moment he looked into the white man's face was that he could hardly make out the features at all. The rage was blinding him, blotting out visual images.

The rage was horrible and violent. *Blind* rage, taking possession of him, of his body and his mind and his very spirit. He beat that white man down in Denver, who was clearly no match for him, beat him senseless, beat him unconscious, beat him to within a bloody inch of his death. And that was why Will ended up spending a year in the Colorado State pen and why he could never fight in the ring again.

He prayed to have that taken from him, that awful anger, and it was. The rage would never overtake him that way again. In time he would, like his brother Mike, become known as "an easygoing fellow." He decided that he would rid himself of alcohol, too. He would stay at home in Idaho from then on, and he would lead a simple, clean life. He wouldn't drink, and he wouldn't fight. It worked for a time. He stayed sober for a number of years. He was still abstinent when he met and married Mary Theresa.

Cecelia didn't know why her father started drinking again, but he did, and her mother grew bitter with the passing years as her condition became worse and worse.

Cecelia hoped her father would not drink that day, that her mother would have a good day and not suffer too much. She would like to come home to them and have them be some kind of company for her. She tried not to think of her father and his drinking or her mother and her craziness and her suffering. She had to get herself prepared to race.

At the St. Mary's track meet, Cecelia fought menstrual cramps as she warmed up, got herself ready for the competition. She hated getting periods. It wasn't fair. She was glad that her shorts were red. She wouldn't have to worry about stains.

Damn cramps. They were very painful; they made her feel queasy, almost like throwing up. It had been like that every time she got her period, ever since she had begun to menstruate six months ago.

The school nurse had given her some Midol tablets before they left Lodi. The school nurse, who was also the "hygiene" teacher, said that menstrual cramps weren't real, though they felt as if they were. They were just imaginary pain. Psychosomatic. It was all in her head—she was resisting becoming a woman. Maybe it was because she didn't want to grow up. She would certainly have resisted if she had thought that it would do her any good. She would have written letters, the way her father did when he ran across situations he didn't like, to her congressman and to editors of newspapers. But there was just no way a person could get out of menstruation, at least none that she knew of or could dream up.

As far as not wanting to be a woman . . . well, if this pain and distasteful messiness were a sample of what being a woman meant (along with being neat, virtuous and hard-working, as her mother said women should be, were expected to be, *were*, if they were normal), then she could certainly live without being a woman. She would be perfectly content to go through life as a preadolescent girl. She would even like it. She could picture herself at seventy-five, white-haired and stooped, but still preadolescent.

Cecelia did push-ups, deep knee-bends, stretching exercises

73

from side to side. She had to loosen those muscles up, get the blood flowing and forget about that awful aching down low in her belly.

She wasn't the tallest, longest-legged one in this competition, although she *was* tall for her age. There was one girl from Coeur d'Alene who looked like some sort of giraffe, tall and skinny and raw-boned, all legs, arms, and neck. Cecelia felt afraid. She had to win this damned race. She just *had* to win. All that training was going to pay off. It would, wouldn't it? Otherwise it would all have been for nothing. Wasted effort. Like her mother's life. Like what her mother always said her life had been.

Cecelia tried to push thoughts of her mother out of her mind, but they kept pushing themselves back in. Mary Theresa had stayed there and lived that hard life because she was the mother of three little girls. That was all. The only reason. Because she had grown to hate her husband. Those girls had one sorry excuse for a father, and she couldn't very well leave them with him. So she was a prisoner until they grew up. She was their mother; she had to be a prisoner.

Mary Theresa told Cecelia that she had lived only for the day when the three little girls were grown-up, and she would be free to leave Will Capture and get away on her own. But just when the last one was nearly grown, when Mary Theresa was forty-three years old and, God knows, older than her years, Cecelia was born.

"And just when I thought I was going to be free, I found out that *you* were on the way." A condemned woman then. Of course, one discrepancy in the story was the boys' births. What about them? She had them one and two years before Cecelia's birth, yet they were always conveniently left out of the story. Mary Theresa had a way, it seemed, of rearranging her memories of how things had been to suit her interpretation of the way things were.

Well, Cecelia was not going to be like that. Never. She didn't know how she would ever manage it, but for certain her life wasn't going to overtake her that way and make her a prisoner and a cripple, miserable, mean and bitter. She would not wind up like her mother. Her life was going to be her own.

74

She *would* be free. Whatever happened to her, however her life turned out, that much was certain. She would be free. She would guide her life through whatever hard times she had to face, and she would end up all right, come what might. Like now. She would win that damned race.

Six schools were competing in the 660. Only six, although seven were in the meet. That meant that someone was sick or injured, or maybe one school didn't have a strong enough runner for the event. The giraffe from Coeur d'Alene was in it, all right. A tall skinny white girl with short curly hair.

Cecelia was the only Indian in her school. She was used to that, but now she was the only Indian *girl* who was competing. There were very few Indians, anyway. She didn't recognize any of them.

Redneck cracker girls. Country girls with freckled faces. Cecelia Capture was going to beat them, she was going to beat them all, just watch, each and every one.

She tried to keep herself calm. The 660 wasn't that important. Not compared to wars and tornados and things like that. But, dammit, winning was. Winning was more important than any war or tornado. Winning was the most important thing in the world.

Her father was the one who had made her go to that white school. Didn't he realize what it would be like? He was always talking about equality and how he loved all mankind. He had been a big football hero when he was going to white school. Of course nobody would discriminate against him under those circumstances. He probably just didn't realize what he was putting her through when he insisted that she go to the Lodi town school instead of the mission school. But he kept telling her it wasn't enough to be as good as. She had to push, push, push, beyond what she thought she could do and become better and smarter and faster and stronger. She remembered again how proud he had been when she skipped third grade. He even had to tell the mailman and Miller down at the grocery store about it. His pride in her had made it seem worthwhile.

The winter she was in fourth grade, a big eighth-grade boy named Jimmy Griffith threw her down the stairs at school. For no reason. Because she was there and he could do it and he thought it would be amusing to do. To him, she was a thing without feelings, like a kitten that young children mistreat; that was how it felt when he grabbed her and carried her, kicking, to the edge of the stairs and threw her down, and he and his friends laughed and then ran away.

Her nose was bruised and swollen. Her nose bled and bled and wouldn't stop. On the bus ride home she used all her Kleenexes and her handkerchief. She was crying, too. She couldn't stop those tears of outrage. This wasn't the first time. Those damned white asses made her life miserable at school all the time. She didn't belong there. They didn't like her being there. She wasn't their kind, and she didn't want to be. She hated them, but all of that was all right because she could beat them at their own game. She could say nothing when they taunted and teased and called her names, or when they ignored her and made her feel as alone as if she were the only person in the world. She could just go on about her business and stay at the head of her class and get herself promoted to a higher grade and then stay at the head of her new class, even though she was a year younger than everyone else. She could get her revenge that way and even things out. But there was nothing she could do about a boy twice her age, twice her size, who could pick her up and throw her down the stairs as a joke.

The bus driver stopped the bus and brought a pack of snow for her to hold against her nose, and at last the bleeding subsided.

Cecelia told her mother, who did nothing but say "Don't you dare tell your father about this. Don't you dare." She told her teacher. She told the principal. Nobody did anything. Jimmy Griffith was the son of a rancher, a man of some influence in the community. Nothing was ever done to him.

Cecelia thought of Jimmy Griffith now and all the town school kids who made her feel like an unwanted misfit. She would break free of them soon enough.

The girls were on their marks for the 660. She wished she could believe in God. Or in a saint. Who was the patron saint of runners?

And then the race began.

She tried to remember to pace herself, but it was no good.

Three girls sprinted on ahead of her, short-legged bundles of energy. They were hardly breathing hard. Regular little rabbits. She would have to let them go for now. Wait for them to tire. No. She was going to spend her energy now. She had to show her stuff. She needed to. Win. Show them up. Win. Beat them. That was all that mattered. Win. Win. Win.

The muscles in her legs burned, but that was all right because she passed them all. She was in the lead now, but it was hard. She began to run with her mouth open. She thought opening her mouth would get more oxygen to her lungs, which felt as if they were about to burst. But running with her mouth open might make her teeth ache. Run. Run. Win. Win.

Her teeth did ache now, and her lungs, and she had a stitch in her side, but she was still ahead. Panting, not pacing herself at all, looking undisciplined, spending all of her energy at once. Win. Win. She concentrated on that one word: winning—but then, almost at the end, the giraffe loped effortlessly ahead of her and kept the lead.

She had a little smile on her face. Her blond curls bounced as she ran. She didn't appear to be out of breath or to have worked up much of a sweat. She wasn't putting all she had into this race, or at least she didn't appear to be, but Cecelia was, and she was beating Cecelia.

Cecelia had nothing in reserve. She had to force her legs to keep running. The race was too short to expect a second wind. Then it was over. The giraffe had won. Of course. The race was over, and Cecelia lay on the grass gasping for breath, her body soaked in sweat, the white T-shirt that said LODI across the chest in red letters stuck wetly to her body. Her lungs ached. Her teeth ached.

It was not bad luck, and it was not a fluke. The giraffe had won because she was a better runner. She had better wind. She was faster. She had more discipline and style, too. There she was over there, her friends gathered around her, winding down from the race.

Cecelia wondered how she would do in cross-country. Cross-country required a great deal of discipline and stamina. The 660, what was that? Mainly nothing but a flashy show of speed. Who was she kidding? She just wasn't that good a runner. She would have to accept it.

Her side still ached. Her stomach was tightening up into a hard ball, into a knotted angry fist inside her body. She would have to forget all that nonsense she had been indulging in about becoming a famous runner. She was no sleek greyhound. She was no gawky giraffe. She was going to have to find another way of winning. Maybe someday she would marry a congressman.

She would have to get up soon. Her sanitary napkin was soaked and had to be changed, and she needed a long cool drink of water. What she hated about it most was not the pain, but the messiness. If it wasn't for that, it would be easier to bear.

By late afternoon, as the school bus headed for home, Cecelia had managed to put her running days behind her. She would no longer compete. She would no longer try. The red ribbon would be just a souvenir of the days when she had wanted to be a runner. That made it not so bad that it was a red ribbon and not a blue one.

The shiny new red ribbon was actually quite likeable and handsome in its way. It said, in fine gold lettering:

SECOND PLACE
GIRLS' 660
Northern Idaho Track
Meet
St. Mary's, Idaho
April, 1962

Her father would be proud when he saw the red ribbon. He would probably tack it to the wall near the Sporting Goods Store calendar and tell everyone he knew that his daughter had won second place at St. Mary's. She had managed to get over the disappointment of not winning first place quite well by the afternoon and looked forward to showing the tangible proof of her accomplishment to her parents.

She could see as soon as she got off the bus that her father was not at home, and her heart sank in disappointment. He was out drinking again, of course, and her mother would be worried, distracted, watching out the window.

Cecelia put the red ribbon in her sweater pocket. She wondered if today had been a good or a bad one for her mother. This wouldn't be a good time to tell her about the track meet, Cecelia thought.

That was the attitude she felt that she *should* have: mild disappointment, sympathetic understanding; Mom suffered so much and Dad, poor fellow, could not help his drinking. That was how she *should* feel, but in reality her face flushed with anger at them both. They were, after all, all she had, and he was a drunk and oblivious most of the time, and it was he who taught her to excel in school and then suddenly stopped caring; so her mother suffered a lot, couldn't she still, even once in a while, through all her suffering, express even a moment's interest in her own daughter? Or, if she could not, couldn't she at least *pretend* that she cared?

It was a lonely, lonely life. In some ways it was even lonelier now for Cecelia, when she was becoming a young woman, than it had been when she was a child. When she was younger she had had her brothers as confidants and companions.

When Cecelia was a little girl she would pretend that her two brothers, who had died as babies, were not really dead. They simply preferred to live with each other somewhere up in the woods behind the house for reasons of their own. She was the only one who knew that the two little graves at the tribal cemetery were empty. She used to meet her brothers clandestinely.

She would go up behind the house a ways, just out of sight in case someone might be watching from a window, and call to them, and they would come running down the slope to meet her. The dogs were in on the game, gleefully barking and wagging their tails in greeting, circling the three siblings as they danced and romped.

She would tell the boys things that had happened and what she had been thinking of, things that worried her. They were perfect brothers, better than any real-life brothers could ever have been.

She wished that she was still able to play games like that, to believe in the two little boys. They would be young men by now, thirteen and fourteen. But she didn't have those brothers, had never really had them, except in her imaginings, so she had no one.

No, this would probably not be a good time to tell her mother about the track meet, she thought, angrily crumpling the stiff red ribbon in her hand inside her sweater pocket, clutching it tightly in her fist.

She found her mother, as she had guessed she would, sitting beside the window, rubbing the swollen knuckles of one hand with the fingers of the other. Her face had its now familiar look of pain, brows pulled together, mouth tense. It was getting so late, she said. She wondered where that man could be.

He was so careless, that man. Probably out drinking again. She hoped nothing bad had happened to him. One of these days he was going to kill himself or someone else with his drunken driving. Oh, how she wished they could get away from this awful, godforsaken place. How she hated it.

Cecelia split kindling, lit a fire in the kitchen stove, began to peel potatoes. She wouldn't cook, though, unless her father came home. Her mother never wanted to eat anymore, at least not meals. All she did was smoke and drink coffee. Cecelia would make herself a peanut butter and jelly sandwich after a while. She sat down in an easy chair near her mother.

She listened to her mother's voice, only tuning in slightly to the words because everything her mother said she had said many times before. Her words recalled her childhood as a railroad man's daughter, and the long, sweet months she spent on her Irish grandparents' farm each year until they died, and the stories her Harrigan grandparents used to tell of Ireland (the old country, they called it) and how it was back in the 1870s in Ireland, the unbearable oppression of Great Britain, whose government confiscated farms and hoarded food and sold the people's own potatoes back to them.

"Then Grandpa Harrigan was caught butchering a hog, *his own hog,* mind you, which he was required to pay a tax on, and since he had tried to get away with not paying the hog-butchering tax, then he would have to pay a fine.

"Grandpa Harrigan killed that British tax man then and there with the same hog-butchering knife he still held in his hand, and then he had to escape, had to run that very night, his underground nationalist buddies helping him.

"A few days later Grandma and her children, my father included—he was born in Killarney—left Ireland with Grandpa's half-brother, whose last name was not the same as theirs, pretending to be the wife and children of Uncle Sean.

"The neighbors all helped Grandma prepare to leave, washing, ironing, sewing, packing. They stayed up all night the night before the day she left. They gave her a gold broach with a pair of manacled hands on it. She always wore it when she got all dressed up to go somewhere. How she would cry sometimes when she spoke of the old country, and say how she would never get to lay eyes on Ireland again, never set foot on Irish soil.

"I always hoped I could go there some day, to Killarney and County Clare and this village, oh, I can't remember the name of it anymore, now let me think, what was it . . . I can't remember the name of the village Grandma was from."

Cecelia had heard it all many times, this Irish talk. She wished her mother did not want to see Ireland. She wished she did not think of herself so much as an Irish person. It was only an accident, after all, that Mary Theresa Harrigan happened to look like her name and was therefore so loved by those two old Irish immigrants who were her grandparents.

What if, instead, Mary Theresa had looked like her own mother, the chief's daughter, or was dark like her own daughters? What if she looked like what she really was, an Indian woman? If she did, she and Cecelia would appear to the world as mother and daughter, and strangers wouldn't have asked, as they so often did when Cecelia was little, if she was adopted (poor little Indian waif, adopted by kindly white people).

Cecelia's Irish forebears were not *her* people. They were *white*, just like the redneck crackers in the little reservation towns, and what would those Irish nationalists named Harrigan back in the

1870s think if they could see her, their great-granddaughter, a wild reservation Indian girl? They had disliked their own daughter-in-law so. Her mother even said that they had, but they tried not to show it.

Would Grandma Harrigan have loved Cecelia? Would Grandma Harrigan, so beloved by Cecelia's mother, have wanted her granddaughter one day to own the prized gold broach with the manacled hands? They were her mother's people maybe. They could never be hers.

"Oh, I don't know what I'll do when you're gone. Do you remember how you used to say when you were little that you would never leave me, that you would stay with me forever and always? And I told you that you would change your mind, and you didn't believe me. *Now* you do, don't you? I can tell. You already think of it. Then I will be all alone here in this hateful house. I wonder if I will be able to walk at all in another few years. It just gets worse and worse. Arthritis is that way. It just gets worse.

"Sometimes, you know, I even, well, begin to wonder if maybe there isn't something wrong with my mind or something. A strange thing happened today. I was sitting here going through these things, reading old letters, old newspaper clippings, looking at photographs. I was tired. I was sleepy, since I had such a bad night last night, kept awake by the pain in my shoulders. I must have fallen asleep, I guess.

"I heard voices coming from the other room, laughing, chattering little voices. I was startled. I didn't know what to think. I could hear them, whoever they were, running around, as if they were chasing each other. I was just about to get up out of my chair and go in there and investigate when they came running in here.

"There were three little girls. I didn't know right at first who they were. Then I recognized them. They were my own little girls, Catherine, Marie and Andrea, all so young and small again. Oh, I was happy. You can't imagine how happy I was.

"They came close to me, and I bent down and stretched out my arms to embrace them, and when I did this I woke myself up. They disappeared. Here I was sitting all alone again, just like before, just like always. The house was so empty. So, so quiet."

Cecelia's mother began to cry.

Cecelia sat across the room and thought of the pathetic little scene her mother had just described, pictured it all, her mother's feelings of expectation as she reached down to embrace the three little girls, and then the cold reality of being old, sick, and all alone.

The struggling, the anger and the despair. When it got to be too much for some, like her father, the flunked-out would-be lawyer, or her great-grandfather, the disinherited Irish nationalist, the anger would explode in awesome violence. Men would be killed with butcher knives or beaten nearly to death, the men unlucky enough to be the ones to deliver that last ounce, the one that would be too much to tolerate, the men whose actions touched off the spark.

And others, like her mother, once the anger and fear became too much, would turn it inward upon themselves and become bent, twisted in body, suffering physical pain and thinking strange, tortured, twisted thoughts.

Her mother's voice began again, and this time it had a different quality. Cecelia recognized the tone. It was cold and mean, full of hatred and bitterness, full of wanting to hurt the one who listened, the one who could not get away and had no choice but to stay and listen.

"Damned dumb Indians. You all think you're something, don't you, you with your pitiful few acres of worthless sand and rock, Indian land that nobody wanted. Royalty, that's what you think you are, you and your father and all you goddamned Captures—what an absurd name that is—and you think I'm just a nobody, don't you, that I ain't got nothin', don't you, Your Royal Highness, that all I am is your servant? Oh, *her.* She's nobody, just something for me to wipe my feet on. You think I don't know that, Your Royal Highness, Miss Oh-So-Smart who skipped third grade, bragging around about your goddamned grades all the time, as if they mattered. Hah. Someone like you, someone who had to pick up beer bottles alongside the road for lunch money, who had to go to school with newspapers lining her shoes. The daughter of a rich man, a landowner, a college-educated person, no less, a girl who is so damned smart she just skipped right by third grade. No wonder you hold yourself, all of you, so far above me, Your Royal Highness.

"I just went to the fifth grade, what do I know? I'm only good enough to give birth to you and then spend my life waiting on you, *you damned dirty cur,* so you can run off to that hick school and show off how smart you are.

"Smart. We'll see about that. We'll see how much good your A's do you when your kids are hungry and the old man's off on a binge with his paycheck. That's real life, Miss High-and-Mighty, not no goddamned report card. Then you'll see how worthless all of that really is and just how worthless you are."

In the light from the fire Cecelia could see her mother's face smiling that familiar, mad smile. She saw her shake her head slowly from side to side, expressing her disgust. She gave a mean, hateful little chuckle to go with the evil smirk.

She was doing *that* again. The way she had when Cecelia was little and they were all alone, the way she had more and more often this past year; she had that strange, evil quality to her voice, as though the real Mary Theresa had gone away.

All Cecelia could do at times like this was to keep quiet and wait for her mother to return to herself. Cecelia was the only one who knew this about Mary Theresa. No friend, no relative, none of her sisters, not her father, no one but herself had ever witnessed the ugly transformation.

Whether it had happened when the others were still at home she didn't know, but it didn't seem likely, somehow. She felt almost sure that this was the result of her mother's long life of anger with no relief and her mother's increasing fear of being left aged and helpless in a place she hated. This was a result of the fear and anger in the same way that the arthritis, Cecelia thought, was a result, a physical manifestation.

Cecelia could see her mother's face briefly when she lit another cigarette; the fire was burning too low by this time to offer any illumination. Her face, in that instant, appeared normal to Cecelia. It's over, then, she thought. It had lasted only a moment this time. The fire burned lower and lower and finally died.

It was so dark all she could see was the dim coal of the lighted cigarette. She watched the red dot of light move as her mother raised the cigarette to her lips. It glowed more intensely for a moment, faded, moved back down. The room grew cold. When her mother spoke again, her voice was like the one she had used when she told of her dream about the three little girls.

"Yes, Grandma never got over having to leave Ireland. She told me so many stories about back in County Clare, it's almost as though her memories became mine. How I wish I could see Ireland just once before I die."

Cecelia wondered, was it that the anger in men turned to murder and violence, and in women to madness?

A coyote in the hills outside howled into the dark, moonless night and was answered by another far away. The sound of the wind was a sighing, lonely sound.

___FOUR

Cecelia, unable to stop the agitation, paced the floor of the cell. She felt foolish, like a cliché of a jailbird. She sat down on the floor with her back against the wall opposite the grey iron door.

If the police interrogated her under a hot lamp, she would sit, stoic and resolute, and not say a word. If they had her cracking rocks with a sledgehammer on a chain gang under a blazing sun, she would show them how strong and durable she was. But this awful isolation was hard to take, this not knowing why she was being kept locked up or how long she would have to stay.

Cecelia wished she had a harmonica (and wished that she could play it, too) so that she could hear some jailhouse songs, like "Swing Low, Sweet Chariot" or the one that went, "Oh, if I had the wings of an angel." She hadn't thought of that song in a long time. She had learned it from her mother. She sang the beginning: "Oh, if I had the wings of an angel, over these prison walls I would fly. I would fly to the arms of my poor darlin', and there I'd be willing to die." The sound of her voice in the empty, silent cell was strange, intrusive. She hummed the tune. She could see herself sitting on the front porch of the old yellow house in Idaho, rocking her Raggedy Ann doll and singing that song. It had been her favorite song. She had believed that she *did* have the wings of an angel, and it would be only a matter of time until she could fly away. That was what her mother had told her.

"What's these sharp things here, Momma? These things sticking up out of my back?" she had asked, twisting an arm behind her so that one hand touched a shoulder blade. She must have been about three at the time.

"Those things? Why, those are your wings."

"Huh-uh. I ain't got no wings."

"Sure you do. What do you think those sharp things are, then, if not folded-up wings?" Cecelia hadn't been able to think of anything. Mary Theresa seldom made jokes. Even now she could not remember a single other instance in which Mary Theresa had told her a story of any kind, except for the ones about Mary Theresa's childhood and those stories that illustrated how unloved and unappreciated she was by everyone. Her mother was not a fanciful, playful sort of person. Cecelia believed that story then and pictured her wings, all folded up tight just beneath her skin.

"Why can't I make 'em come out so I can use 'em to fly around?"

"Because you're not grown-up yet. Now your wings only unfold while you're sleeping. As soon as you wake they go right back in their hiding place."

"Have you ever seen 'em?"

"Sure."

"What do they look like?"

"They're pretty wings with white feathers. Like the wings of an angel."

Cecelia didn't know when she quit believing that she had wings. As a child she often dreamed of flying and imagined sometimes that she really did fly around while everyone else slept. She looked forward eagerly to the day when she would be grown and acquire full-time use of her wings.

She thought that her favorite song must have been made up by a little girl like herself, another secret angel, who had been imprisoned, and when she sang, "Oh, if I had the wings of an angel, over these prison walls I would fly," the girl was wishing she had the use of her wings right then, instead of having to wait until she was grown-up to fly over the walls and escape.

Cecelia tried to remember the Mary Theresa who told the angel story, but she could not. That memory was the only one of its kind, it seemed. She remembered her mother as a cold, distant woman, always suffering, always complaining, sitting by the window smoking and watching the highway as she awaited Will Capture's drunken return. That was how she had been when they still lived out in the country in Idaho, when she spoke so often of getting old and dying and how she longed to leave that place, how she longed to be closer to her other daughters and to have a better, less lonely, easier life.

They did leave, finally, Cecelia and her mother and father, in the early summer of the year Cecelia was twelve. They packed up their things and they left the place where both Cecelia and her father were born, and they went to live in Tacoma, Washington. She remembered how it had been and thought how things could be worse. Instead of being in jail she could be in Tacoma.

_Five

Tacoma was old and seedy, decaying, full of factories, refineries, pulp mills, sailors and soldiers. It always smelled like skunk in Tacoma. The business district was one big skid row, and the city sprawled out in all directions: used-car lots, shopping centers, fast-food restaurants, the B&I Circus Store and on and on. Unbearably ugly. Urban sprawl with a vengeance.

The rain poured down, and the pink corpses of earthworms appeared on the pavement.

School was not like school back home in Idaho. It was a place to keep students off the streets, a sort of holding tank for tough, inner-city whites and cool, bad, shuckin' and jivin' blacks. Cecelia kept a low profile and studied and read and sought escape at the library. Blacks and whites, she was foreign to them all. Her father, who spoke often of racial equality, told her this story when she was a very little girl:

"One day, up in heaven, in fact the day after He finished creating the earth, God was puttering around in His kitchen and got to thinking how lonely He was and how someone ought to live on the earth. So He got the idea of creating a person.

"He took some holy bread dough and fashioned a person and

put the person in the oven to bake. God was a bit overeager, though, and jumped the gun on this one. His first person was not done. It was all pale, almost like raw dough.

" 'Damn!' God said and tossed this first effort out.

"God made a second person and popped it into the oven.

" 'This time I'll let it bake a good, long time,' He said, which He did. Too long. The second person was burned black and also had to be thrown out.

"God then made a third person and put this one inside the oven. This time God was very careful not to either underbake or burn this person. When He opened the oven door the third time, a person emerged who was done just right, a fine, beautiful brown.

" 'By golly,' He said, 'I'm going to call you Indian. You and those other two, White-Eyes and Negro, will share the earth. You have a good time down there and be sure and pray often, all three of you.'

"And that is the true story of how God created Man."

The implication was that God Himself was Indian, and that was how Cecelia would picture Him, an old Indian man with long white braids and a black Stetson hat, moccasins and baggy pants with suspenders. God was a bachelor, fond of puttering around His house and yard, the type who might bake some persons. That was the God she would pray to during Mass and in the confessional when she crossed herself and said, "Bless me, Father, for I have sinned."

Alone in a strange concrete wilderness of black and white only, except for herself and her father and God, Cecelia turned to the Tacoma Public Library. She checked out countless teenage books, then branched out. She read *Gone with the Wind*, which led to *The Red Badge of Courage*, which led to a couple of history books about the Civil War and then a biography of ex–confederate soldier Jesse James, who robbed only Yankee Pullman cars and banks.

The library was a wonderful place. A retreat. A refuge. Peace, serenity, quiet, law and order.

It was a good thing, her mother often said, that Cecelia had learned to read; otherwise she would do absolutely nothing, useless thing that she was, of no earthly good to herself or anyone else. She was not like the two oldest sisters, Catherine and Marie, such hardworking girls, who had brought joy into their mother's life, not pretty like them, either; why, when they were young girls and still living at home they were highly sought-after. Lots of friends, lots of suitors. Nobody had ever liked Cecelia very much. She was so odd. She didn't talk much, just sat around all the time. She wasn't at all lively. She gave her mother the willies sometimes.

Back in Idaho her mother would watch her on the slope behind the house, where she apparently thought no one could see her, talking to the air as if other people were there. She would talk and talk and laugh and dance, spin round and round until she fell dizzily on the ground. Her mother wondered, then, about demons, but would make the sign of the cross and push such thoughts away. She would tell Catherine and Marie about seeing Cecelia talking to the air but she did not bring up the subject with Cecelia until she was quite grown. It became one of her "You-were-such-a-funny-kid" stories.

No man would ever have her, her mother told her, not ever. She was destined to live a solitary life, prowling the stacks of some musty public library, losing herself in books because she was too backward to be with real people. She could live her life in a pretend world. She could even go off and rob banks with Jesse James himself. In fact, she would have to, since no real-life man would ever want her.

The apartment, on the edge of a black section of town, smelled of mothballs and God knew what else. It was long and narrow, with the living room, kitchen, and one bedroom all in a straight line. The only windows were in the front, at the far end of the living room, and in the back bedroom, where Will Capture slept.

There was not enough light in the apartment. Its walls were covered with brown wallpaper, and naked light bulbs hung from the ceiling. Metal TV trays bought at the Salvation Army served as utility tables.

At thirteen Cecelia began to wear a bra (though she had put that off as long as possible) and to think of herself as a woman instead of a child. She longed for her own room, longed for privacy, but she had to share a bed with her mother. The bed folded into the wall during the day and folded out into the living room at night. Her mother would sit on the edge and watch late movies on TV while Cecelia tried to sleep.

Her father had the privacy of his own room, way in back, where he could go when he came home drunk, stumbling up the side stairway in the night. He could go there to lie down and sober up. He could go there to look out the window at the city and think about things. He could listen to the news station on his radio, and he could read his books and papers and write letters to the editors of newspapers and to the tribal council and to people he knew back in Idaho. Cecelia envied him and wondered if he knew what a good life he was living. It was a good thing for both of them that they had learned to read.

Her mother seemed happier than she had been back in Idaho. She didn't complain about her arthritis so much any more. She had TV and her two oldest daughters and all her little grandchildren nearby, to visit and call up on the telephone, and neighbors to chat with out in the hallway.

Life was easier now than ever before, away from the damned dumb Indians and back to civilization, with a laundry room in the basement of the building that had automatic, coin-operated washing machines and clothes driers. Yet her behavior toward Cecelia did not improve.

She would tell Catherine and Marie how awful it was. Cecelia acted rude to her. Cecelia would not wash a dish or pick up a broom without being told. Why, she would actually sit there reading while her poor old ailing mother scrubbed the floor. Catherine and Marie and the third sister, Andrea, who lived on the other side of the mountains, and their mother formed a tight family circle of their own, and Cecelia and her father were thoroughly excluded.

They hated Cecelia for her laziness, and she *was* lazy. She was lazy both consciously and deliberately. She was uncompromising in her laziness. It was absolutely true that she would not do a lick of work without being told. But then she would do it without telling her mother that she was a horrible wretch and she wished she would die. But she did protest silently by being lazy.

She knew by experience that nothing she could do would ever please her mother, so she refused to try. She did not aspire to be a "hardworking girl" like her sisters. She would not accept her mother's system of values. She rejected the formula: Housework equals virtue, womanly virtue. The harder one worked, the shinier the floor, the more dishes washed, the better the woman who had done the work. If she accepted that, she would lose all sense of herself, be completely cast adrift and at her tyrant-mother's mercy. Her laziness was a point of honor, a way of asserting her independence.

So her mother would tell Catherine and Marie, and they would agree with her that their sister was incorrigible and it was too bad she had to be around at all, such a terrible burden she was, and their mother had worked so hard all her life and deserved an easier time of it now that she was getting old, too bad they couldn't send her to Reman Hall, Tacoma's juvenile detention center. It wasn't enough, though, that she was just incorrigible and lazy.

She should be sent away to a government-run Indian boarding school. That would shape her up fast, take the wind out of her sails. No more lazing around for her. She should be sent to Kansas or Oklahoma or South Dakota. She should be sent somewhere far away.

They helped their mother send away to the Bureau of Indian Affairs for application forms, which Cecelia refused to sign. Government schools were for academic underachievers, or for Navajos or Apaches who had lived in the heart of the reservation all their lives and could not speak English and knew nothing of white ways. You learned a trade if you were lucky. If you were not, you learned how to be a housemaid. You learned how to get along in the world, more or less. You learned to live like a reasonable facsimile of a white person. That was what her father always said about government boarding schools. Government school didn't interest her any more than being a martyr did.

Kansas. Oklahoma. South Dakota. None of those places appealed to her, either. She would not allow herself to be "sent away." When she chose to go away, she would. She was a person in her own right. Nobody could "send her away." But she didn't wish to argue. She only said that she would not sign the forms.

Somehow more than a year passed in Tacoma, and Cecelia was thirteen and a half and it was the fall of the year. She hated Tacoma still, would always hate it and the junior high school that was like a holding tank and the musty little apartment.

Cecelia sat at the window watching the rain hitting the pavement on the street, watching the shine of the puddles of water below the street lights.

"By God," her mother vowed, pacing back and forth with heavy steps and wringing her hands, "I wish I could leave. Just up and leave. Right now."

Her mother often talked of leaving. She who had never worked, who was in her late fifties and suffered from arthritis. She talked about leaving her husband and taking care of both herself and Cecelia, getting a job and a place of her own. She would never get state aid, though. She thought welfare was disgraceful. She would almost rather die than go on welfare.

Her mother said if she had the money, she would get on the bus and go to Wapato. Wapato was a small town just over the mountains, where Cecelia's third sister, Andrea, lived with her husband and baby. Andrea, it seemed, was the daughter her mother had a special feeling for. Andrea was the one she wished she could be around. Andrea's baby's middle name was Theresa, and her mother liked to think that the baby looked like her, although she really bore no resemblance to her whatsoever. Living in Tacoma, Mary Theresa didn't get to see Andrea and the baby girl often enough to suit her. That was why, if she had enough money, she would get on the bus and go to Wapato.

Cecelia considered. Wapato. Population 4,000. Located on the Yakima Indian Reservation. The Yakima Valley had no urban sprawl, just little towns dotting the countryside. She liked it in Wapato. Before Andrea moved there, they had gone once in a while when she was little for the White Swan All-Indian Rodeo and celebration.

94

Many, many Indians lived there, and lots of Mexicans who had originally come to work in the fields had ended up making the valley their home. Brown-skinned people again. If they went there, they would be out of Tacoma. Cecelia would have friends, maybe, a place where she belonged. Brown people. Real people. No more all-white or all-black. Black and white. So odd. The way some people dreamed. A place of stark extremes. A foreign country. Sometimes, when her father was drunk, he would say that he was not at all bothered by white/black, since he "loved all mankind." To her Tacoma was a foreign country. Always.

This could be her opportunity, if handled right.

"Hey, Mom," Cecelia said, "I have some money." She had been secretly saving up to buy a good winter coat when the weather got really bad, a fancy imported raincoat, not just a make-do discount-store special.

"You? You have money?" her mother asked suspiciously. "And where, might I ask, did you get this money?" She should have thought of an answer beforehand. It was largely embezzled from the money she was given when she went to the store for family groceries.

"I saved it up, Mom. From my lunch money." This was also true. "You know, I have been on a diet and not eating lunch lately. And I just had a feeling that maybe you and I might be needing that money. That it just might come in handy."

"Oh." Mary Theresa stopped, and her puffy face looked thoughtful. "How much?"

"Nearly forty dollars."

"Well, Cece, I just don't know. I wonder how it would work out."

"Just fine, I'm sure. You said if you only had the money, Mom. You've got it."

Cecelia's father was gone at the time, drinking again, which was the reason her mother felt like leaving.

"Okay. Come on, then. Let's get packed up and leave. Phone the bus depot, will you, and find out when the next bus leaves."

There was a pan of baked chicken being kept warm for dinner in the oven. Cecelia wrapped several pieces in aluminum foil and put them in a brown paper bag. She was going to be glad to see the last of this place. She was happy to be going. Her father would be all right, and she would write him later on.

"*What* are you *doing?*" her mother asked accusingly.

"I'm wrapping some chicken to take along. In case we get hungry later tonight."

"Always thinking of eating, aren't you," her mother said tiredly, "always thinking of stuffing your face." She shook her head sadly. But on the bus that night, as they were crossing over the summit, Mary Theresa ate heartily of the chicken her daughter had brought along.

It was daylight when they reached Wapato, and already the day was hot, almost uncomfortably so. They didn't know exactly where to begin looking for Andrea.

Mary Theresa sighed. "First let's have some breakfast," she said, and Cecelia thought that maybe her mother had some money in addition to the forty dollars she had given her, since their bus fare had come to twenty dollars for the two of them.

They went looking for a place that was open, Cecelia carrying two shopping bags filled with belongings, her mother a large, battered brown suitcase secured with a belt around its middle because it would not stay closed any other way. In the all-night café they found Andrea, waiting tables. She was surprised to see them.

"What are you guys doing here?"

"We left him," Cecelia said.

Andrea was her mother's favorite child because she had had tuberculosis as a child and teenage girl and had spent years in the sanitarium and at home recuperating. Everyone knew how TB patients could go. They would seem perfectly healthy, fully recovered, and then they would hemorrhage in the night and be gone. Just like that.

Andrea had had to be watched and worried over, and whenever her mother spoke a harsh word to her, a thought cut across her mind: She might be dead tomorrow. And so she always did her best to treat Andrea well. She still worried about her, about her health, even though now the part of her lung that had been affected had been surgically removed, and she had been well for years.

Andrea brought their breakfast and sat down in their booth with a cup of coffee of her own.

"So, what are you going to do?" she asked her mother.

"Oh, I don't rightly know, Andrea. Get myself some kind of a job, of course. I guess."

"I see," Andrea said. Her mother was in her late fifties. She often talked of working—in the fruit-packing sheds maybe, as a chambermaid in a hotel, as a cleaning woman in a nursing home. But her knees and back were bad, and she had no Social Security card, anyway.

"Why did you leave, Ma? What was it?"

"Don't you know? Can't you guess? The same old razzamatazz as always. Only worse now that he doesn't work steady anymore. He has more time on his hands these days—more time to think up insulting things to say, more time to drink and perform around. Found one of his old high school football pals in Tacoma. That one also, conveniently, is an alcoholic. No more of that for me. I'm through!"

"I see," Andrea said quietly. "Well, Ma, I've got to get back to work now."

Andrea looked up at the big electric clock on the wall above the door. Almost eight. She gave them directions how to get to her place: down across the tracks, turn left at the Crossroads Market, down the gravel road to the cabin court at the edge of town. The baby was at the babysitter's cabin, the first one as you turn into the court.

"It must get high, paying a babysitter," her mother commented.

"Yes."

"Well, now I'm here. I can help out and watch her for you."

"Yes."

"Dear, are you *all right?*" Andrea's face seemed drained of color.

"Yes, Mother."

"You don't look well at all." It turned out later that Andrea was pregnant again. She would usually be pregnant throughout her twenties.

"Truly, Ma, I'm fine, really. Now go on, you guys. I've got to run. See you around four, okay?" She smiled and stood up from the booth, ending the conversation.

It was a long walk from the café to the cabin court, and very hot. The shopping bags were heavy, and the handles cut into the palms of Cecelia's hands.

After they crossed the tracks and passed the potato-packing shed, they could see open fields—brown, plowed, empty fields stretching two miles or more to the new highway, orchards of peach and cherry on the other side, and beyond them the high, yellow-red velvet hills.

WELCOME TO THE BEAUTIFUL, BOUNTIFUL YAKIMA VALLEY, a big sign had said as they came down out of the mountain pass. Behind the lettering a horn of plenty spilled out luscious fruits and vegetables. A few miles down the way, on the other side of the city of Yakima, another sign had announced, NOW ENTERING THE YAKIMA INDIAN RESERVATION, HOME OF THE UNITED TRIBES AND BANDS OF THE YAKIMA NATION. Cecelia's spirits had risen when she read that sign. Things were going to be better from then on. She knew it.

The Yakima Valley. She would have to try to make it work out. It would just be a matter of time before her mother began hating it and saying she couldn't stand being around "damned dumb Indians." Cecelia would have to do something to prevent a return to Tacoma. She put down the shopping bags and breathed deeply. Fresh air at last, hot, still, dry fresh air. It smelled good.

"Hurry up," her mother called, not stopping, not turning around. She trudged on ahead with her head down.

Cecelia picked up the two bags again. She hoped it wasn't much farther or her hands would blister. She was sweating now. The sun was beginning to beat down. It wouldn't be rainy here, as it was over on the coast, in Tacoma. She hurried to catch up with her mother.

The cabin court came into view about half a mile or more down the road—six small, recently whitewashed cabins, one-room affairs with tar-papered roofs and small porches. Tall trees rose up around the circle of cabins, offering a lot of shade. There was no grass growing anywhere nearby, only dust, thick dry white dust.

Several dogs lay sleeping near one of the cabins. Cecelia wondered where she and her mother would sleep. Andrea's car, probably. She wondered how much hotter the day would get.

___SIX

The summer of 1963 had been a hot one in the Yakima Valley. That was what everyone said. Some said the temperature got up to 103 degrees. Others said 105, but they could remember back in fifty-two or fifty-three it had been much hotter than that: 110 or thereabouts. Anyway, by late August, everyone agreed, the worst was already over, and they told Cecelia and Mary Theresa they would really know heat when summer came again, and this 92-degree August was nothing, just nothing, compared with what it had been and would be again. Just wait, they said.

At first, for two weeks or three, Mary Theresa and Cecelia did sleep in Andrea's car at the cabin court. They babysat during the day and washed diapers and other laundry by hand in a round metal tub and hung the wash out to dry on a wire line stretched between the cabins, and they were wretchedly poor for a time.

Cecelia didn't mind so much being wretchedly poor because she was just thirteen and Wapato was a welcome change from Tacoma. Later on, whenever she drove past the cabin court on the old river road highway, she would remember the sweltering August heat in the poorly insulated cabin and the refried beans and tortillas, which was all Andrea cooked for her Mexican husband; and she would remember the flies early in the morning sleeping black and ugly on the ceiling before the heat woke them and they began to buzz alive.

Mary Theresa loved caring for her curly-haired baby granddaughter, loved hugging her and kissing the dimpled face and bathing and powdering her and dressing her up in crisp, cool, cotton dresses. Mary Theresa and the baby girl, Theresa, were clearly ecstatic to have each other.

Mary Theresa fretted about not having money and said she would have to find herself a job. She said that every evening, almost like a ritual, when supper was over and the dishes washed. She would look out across the fields, past the railroad tracks, her eyes fixed upon the tallest structure in town: the gleaming aluminum water tower with the word WAPATO painted on it in tall black letters, and as this water tower reflected the day's last bit of rosy amber sunlight, Mary Theresa would say, "I must find a job. Somehow I must. Maybe tomorrow."

Field work was plentiful, but of course Mary Theresa couldn't do such strenuous labor, not in her condition and in the awful heat.

One day Andrea came home and said that her boss at the café had told her to ask her sister if she wanted a job waitressing. Andrea laughed, and so did her mother. It was a joke. Ha ha, imagine Cecelia working at the café. Andrea said she told her boss that her sister was just thirteen, and he said he had thought she was probably sixteen or seventeen. It was funny. To Andrea and her mother it was a joke. Ridiculous. To Cecelia, though, it was a sweet, precious notion.

I look sixteen or seventeen, she would think to herself at night while she lay in the front seat of Andrea's little Ford coupé looking up through the open window at the stars.

The thought would fill her with a warm glow. I look sixteen or seventeen, and if it weren't for Andrea and her big mouth, I could have a job and money and a car and be self-supporting. Sometimes she would fall asleep daydreaming about this, about what it would be like to have her own apartment and her own car and to be regarded as grown-up and independent even though she was just thirteen, and how all that would be possible were it not for prejudice against young people.

Sometimes in the early evening Cecelia and one of the neighbors in the cabin court, an eighteen-year-old unmarried welfare mother named Donna, who was from Missouri, would walk down the road to the Crossroads Market. Donna would buy Cokes for herself and Cecelia, and love books and movie magazines, which Cecelia would be allowed to read.

On these occasions boys would pass them in cars and whistle. If traffic was light enough, the boys would sometimes slow their cars and drive alongside the girls and ask them what their names were and did they want a ride. Cecelia and Donna wouldn't speak to them, but they both enjoyed the attention, and Cecelia would smile and think to herself: Yes, I do look sixteen or seventeen and what's more I am becoming devastatingly attractive to boys.

In the evenings, after the sun went down, someone would "water down the premises" with a hose, and the fine, dry dust would settle and everything took on a cool, neat appearance.

Mary Theresa and a band of several old ladies would gather under one of the trees, setting up folding chairs on the damp, neat ground. They would roll their own smokes with Bull Durham tobacco and zigzag papers and sit for hours, talking and smoking, enjoying one another's company and the cool of the night after the hot, hot day.

Cecelia would sit with Donna on the porch of the cabin Donna shared with her toddler son and older brother, who worked in the fields and could not read and could only print his name, which was Clarence.

Cecelia had no stories of her own to tell, so she sat and listened as Donna told tales of love and pain and adventure that were sometimes suspiciously similar to the stories they both read in *True Confessions.*

They played Donna's radio, which blared forth the Everly Brothers' hits, "Wake Up, Little Suzie" and "Bye, Bye, Love" mostly. It was the Everly Brothers, anyway, that Cecelia remembered about that summer at the cabin court and her short-lived, strange friendship with Donna, whom she had considered so worldly.

Donna and she would apply red or shocking-pink nail polish to their fingernails and toenails, and sometimes Donna would rat Cecelia's hair and do it up in a beehive hairdo, which she then sprayed and pinned into place. Donna gave Cecelia her own can of hair spray. Donna, who was the only person on welfare in the court, seemed to have more money than anyone else and was therefore greatly resented by the others.

Cecelia enjoyed Donna's Missouri drawl and began speaking sometimes with a slight southern accent herself. She stopped abruptly after she addressed Mary Theresa as "Momma" in that southern drawl one day, asking her, "Momma, have y'all seen mah hair spray?" Mary Theresa's face reddened, and she was, for once, at a loss for words. Finally she spat out, "Don't you *ever* talk like that again. You sound like some piece of white trash." That was the end of Cecelia's Missourian accent.

Mary Theresa found a halftime job selling light bulbs by telephone for a dollar an hour. It wasn't enough, of course, but Cecelia was impressed with Mary Theresa and Mary Theresa with herself that she had found a job at all. When she got her first paycheck she took Cecelia to the movies and out for a Chinese dinner. Her appearance improved and her disposition, and for a while it seemed as though even her physical ailments were improving.

Then Mary Theresa "secured a position" as a housekeeper-companion to a senile woman in her eighties. Mary Theresa and Cecelia again had to sleep in the same bed, and Cecelia missed the relative privacy of the front seat of Andrea's car, but it was a neat, comfortable little house, and in addition to room and board, Mary Theresa was paid fifty dollars a month cash and given Sundays off. The "board" was good, too, with plenty of meat and fruit and vegetables. Mary Theresa was really providing for them, after all, as she had said she would when they left Tacoma.

When school began, Cecelia had a new sweater and a pair of shoes bought at Savin' Sandy's just outside of Toppenish, which asked, on the sign beneath its name, "Why pay more for a purty store?" Savin' Sandy's was within the boundaries of the reservation, unlike the township, and therefore Indians did not have to pay state sales tax at Sandy's.

Except for the new blue sweater and the white pumps, Cecelia's clothes were worn and shabby, but they still fit because she hadn't grown in the past year, which pleased her a great deal. She was, in fact, even a bit thinner going on fourteen than she had been the year before.

The school at Wapato was about half white and the rest either Mexican or Indian. There was no black child. The lone black man in Wapato was called Mophead by the teenagers because of his long kinky hair, which he wore in little braids all over his head. He could be seen going about town pulling a rusty little red wagon behind him. He scavenged garbage cans behind stores and restaurants for his food and picked up beer and soda pop bottles to sell. Mophead was very black, and his clothes were very dirty. People pretended not to see him. One of Cecelia's friends told her that some boys had followed Mophead home one day and found that he lived in a little shack down by the river made of old tin signs and scrap wood. Of course, those boys were known to lie. Nobody really knew anything about Mophead.

Cecelia fit in easily with the Indians and quickly made friends. Sarah, Tillie, Ramona, LaVonne and Cecelia soon formed a tight little group that would remain together throughout the Wapato years. Cecelia was happy now, but sometimes she missed her father and hoped that he was doing all right. She knew she would see him again, when the time came.

Cecelia was in junior high school now. For the first time in her life since beginning school, academic excellence had no meaning for her. Her friends were not academic achievers and didn't value anyone who was. They liked giggling and passing notes and stopping at the teenage hangout on the way home from school to eat french fries with gobs of ketchup and drink Cokes and dance the chicken and the stroll and smoke cigarettes. Cecelia learned how to blow smoke rings. Academic achievement was not expected of her anymore, and she didn't care at all. She gladly put aside all thoughts of books and schoolwork. Belonging was better than any of that could ever be.

Mary Theresa grew to hate the senile old woman who was now her charge. The old lady stole her own silverware and hoarded it under stacks of clothes in a dresser drawer. She would forget who Cecelia and Mary Theresa were and then be alarmed when she woke to find two strangers wandering around her house. Each morning Mary Theresa and Cecelia had to reintroduce themselves to her and explain just what it was they were doing there. "That crazy old bat," as Mary Theresa called her, had to be watched constantly lest she wander away or get into some mischief.

The crazy old bat had to be dressed and have her hair combed for her. She even had to be assisted in bathing. All this and cooking, cleaning and listening to the prattle of the old woman was too much for Mary Theresa to bear. She was being driven mad, she told Cecelia every day. She had headaches, she developed what she thought must surely be an ulcer, and worst of all, her arthritis flared up again.

At last, when it was almost winter, Mary Theresa told Cecelia that she had come to the end of her rope. She wrote a letter to her husband, offering reconciliation if he would promise to stop drinking, which he, of course, quickly agreed to do.

Will Capture then did something he always said he would never do: he sold a one-hundred-acre parcel of land. Cecelia remembered he had always said that that land contained the bones of countless generations of ancestors and was of far greater value than money. She knew how hard it was for him to part with that land. They needed a house, however, and had no money and no other way of getting any, now that Will was too old to work. He wanted to do what was right, he said, and he took the proceeds from the sale of the land and purchased a rundown old three-bedroom house on Wasco Avenue that had a beautiful old tree growing in its yard. He could fix it up, he said, build a new porch, repair the roof, scrape off the peeled green paint and paint it a gleaming new white. He did all these things, too, and cleared the overgrown yard, pulled all the weeds and cut the grass and watered it until it grew green again. In the early winter of 1964, the Capture family moved into the house on Wasco Avenue in Wapato, Washington, and Mary Theresa's career as an independent working woman came to an end.

SEVEN

Jail was not so bad any more, not the way it was at first. Cecelia did not feel so frantic. It was as if she had slowed down her thoughts, her breathing, everything. Even the blood in her veins seemed to have slowed down in response to being jailed, to have somehow adjusted to this new condition. She no longer felt an urgent need to do something. She had, for the time being, anyway, accepted the situation.

Maybe that was the way it was with everything, or with most things. Her labor pains, when she had Corey, were horribly, searingly painful. She felt as if she were being torn in half. The doctors in the labor room at San Francisco General didn't believe that she was suffering so much, and she tried to be brave, but the labor went on hour after hour after hour. Relentless, punishing, wrenching. Cecelia didn't know how she or anyone could bear such pain and still live. She cried in agony. She pleaded with the doctors to help her, to give her something to ease the pain, to knock her out, to do something, for God's sake. But they ignored her or talked to her as if she were six years old. "Now you're having a baby. You have to expect a little pain. It hurts to have a baby. All women must go through a little pain when they have babies." But it was not a little pain. It was not.

She overheard one of the doctors telling a young medical student not to mind her. "She's just a young kid. Unmarried. From the home. They get like that sometimes. Just scared is all. Don't mind her. She's okay." She wadded part of her sheet and put it in her mouth and bit her teeth into it as hard as she could to keep from screaming, and she hoped to God that that doctor was right, that nothing was wrong.

Years later, when she gave birth to Nicole and experienced normal childbirth, she knew positively that that first labor was all wrong. It was in no way normal. The pains of that labor were nothing like the ones she went through with Nicole. They were not only dreadfully sharp, they were that way from the very beginning.

The doctors changed shifts, and an impatient young intern took over. He reached his gloved hand up inside her body, near the part where she was hurting most, and said she hadn't dilated. Hardly at all.

"This is ridiculous," he said through his surgical mask, his eyebrows drawn together in an annoyed expression. "This is taking much, much too long. I'm going to rupture the membrane." It was almost twenty-four hours after labor had started when he decided to do that. He took a pair of scissors with long blades to cut the bag of waters open, and it was while he was doing this that he discovered that there was no bag of waters, and that was why it was all taking so long.

"Why didn't you tell us that the bag of waters had broken?" they demanded. She didn't know. How was she supposed to know? They shook their heads in disgust. It was her fault. She was stupid.

By the time the broken bag of waters was discovered, Cecelia had stopped suffering so much. Though she still felt the pain, she had in some way got used to it. It had become a part of her. She had transcended it. She quietly observed the proceedings as they began an IV to induce labor and took her into the delivery room.

Then she gave birth, and the absence of the pain was an odd feeling.

They laid the baby boy on an examining table right across from her head. He was all sticky, covered with blood, which dried quickly; his black hair was matted and plastered down with the blood, and he appeared to be dead.

"What's wrong with him?" she asked as they drew mucus from his nose and mouth with a little syringe. They ignored her. "What's wrong with my baby? Is he dead?"

He didn't move, and he didn't breathe. The doctor motioned in Cecelia's direction, and one of the nurses put herself in Cecelia's line of vision and told her to turn her head. The last she had seen they were pushing on the baby's chest.

Later she asked them how long it had been before Corey took a breath, and they told her only seconds, that he had begun to breathe before two minutes. But to her, at the time, it seemed to be twenty minutes or more that she lay there, wondering about it all and not trusting the doctors and feeling afraid. At last she heard the thin, sickly little cry begin, and in no time at all it grew louder and stronger and became an angry, healthy cry.

To look at Corey Donahue today, no one would ever know that he had been such a skinny, sickly baby, a baby who had seemed to be dead when he was born. Corey was only thirteen, but he was already as tall as his mother and very strong, healthy and well-coordinated. Cecelia wondered how her boy was, how he was doing up there in Spokane without her now. She missed him terribly; she missed both of her children. The sound of the clanging keys and the lock turning startled her. The door opened and a neat young woman in a green cardigan sweater, green plaid skirt and crisp white blouse stepped into her cell. She looked like a Catholic schoolgirl as she peered at Cecelia through wire-rimmed glasses. She was a serious, earnest-looking girl.

"Ms. Welles? How do you do? I'm Susan Fletcher from the public defender's office. I'm here to determine your eligibility for representation by our office. I need to ask you a few questions." She perched herself on the edge of the lower bunk, holding a clipboard on her knees, and poised a pen over the forms clipped onto the board.

The interview went very quickly. The questions were few and very direct, very simple. They were especially simple because Cecelia simplified them by lying. She wanted to be eligible for the public defender's services so she said she owned no house, no property, no assets at all, except an old broken-down automobile.

She was divorced, had been for years. She was living on a $500-per-month scholarship from the university (this much was true). She wanted to leave Nathan out of this. She couldn't allow him such ammunition. He found fault with her where there was no fault. What would he do with this?

"A lawyer will be around to see you soon, Ms. Welles. Probably tomorrow morning. They only do interviews in the morning."

"Tomorrow?" Cecelia said. "Not today?"

"Tomorrow," Susan said, rapping on the door to be let out. "Oh, I'm sorry. It can't be tomorrow. Tomorrow is Saturday. Monday morning, then."

"Why not until tomorrow or Monday? Why are they doing this to me? Shouldn't I be out on OR by now? Why are they keeping me here?"

Susan looked at her directly for the first time. They could hear someone with keys moving down the hall.

"Why are they keeping you here? Do you mean that nobody told you?"

Cecelia could feel panic rising in her. "No. Nobody told me. I'm asking you to tell me. What the hell is going on?"

Susan Fletcher paused a moment, took a breath. They could hear the sound of the door being unlocked, then opening.

"You're being held because of an old warrant dating back to 1972. You mean you weren't told?"

Cecelia shook her head dumbly.

"Welfare fraud," Susan said. "Bond has been set at twenty-five thousand dollars. They were supposed to have told you." She added this last in an annoyed tone.

This was worse than anything Cecelia could have imagined if she had allowed herself to imagine anything at all. It was overwhelming. She didn't notice Susan's leaving, or the door being closed again. Susan simply wasn't there anymore. She turned into vapor after delivering those awful lines, and Cecelia was left by herself with this dreadful new knowledge.

It didn't seem possible. That old ghost from another lifetime had finally caught up with her. She had successfully evaded justice for ten years, but she hadn't escaped as she thought she had after all.

Cecelia wanted a cigarette badly. Even one of those menthol brands. She would have paid twenty dollars for a cigarette. She lay on the upper bunk on her back and stared at the ceiling. Such a high ceiling for such a small room. She stared at the poor, dim overhead light, and she remembered what her life had been like before Berkeley and before Nathan . . . way, way back to the days when she was a teenage welfare mother. She was unmarried and poor, a high school dropout with no skills and a little boy to raise all by herself. She didn't like to remember that period of her life.

Seventeen. Eighteen. Nineteen. Those were her welfare-mother years, which she had sometimes thought might go on forever. Welfare did go on forever for some people. Being unskilled, uneducated, dependent upon the state welfare system for support had become a deeply ingrained way of life for many of the welfare mothers she met during that time.

Was that really her, ragtag young girl that she was, dragging her baby around to seedy apartments in San Francisco's Mission District or Western Addition or the Fillmore?

Welfare City. Sometimes she worked, but the little jobs that she was able to get, clerical jobs or waitressing jobs, paid less than what she got from the welfare, once she had paid a sitter. It hurt her now to remember the squalor of her background, hers and Corey's. Dead-end low-paying jobs and then back to Welfare City.

Once, yearning for the companionship of other Indians, Cecelia had gone to the American Indian Center over on Sixteenth Street. She was singularly unimpressed with it, a shabby, rundown suite of rooms up a dark flight of stairs in a skid-row section of town. No one was up there except a couple of disreputable-looking men playing pool.

She went into an Indian bar on South Van Ness, stood at the crowded bar and ordered herself a beer, which they served her even though she was only eighteen. But as it turned out, she didn't even stay long enough to finish the beer.

There were Indians there, all right, lots of Indians from all over the country, and most of them were already drunk, though it was still very early. These Indians were, it seemed to her, hopeless, displaced people. No longer Indian, yet not white either. Big-city Indians talking about how great it was "back home on the rez," banding together, a band of outcasts. They began conversations by asking what the other's tribe was. Arapahoe, Cheyenne, Navajo, Cherokee, Sioux, it didn't matter.

A little old man, very drunk, in a long black overcoat, asked Cecelia what her tribe was. She ignored him as best she could.

"What's your tribe, sweetheart? What's your tribe? Huh? Oh, not talkin', eh? I know what tribe you are—you're like me, that's what you are, that's okay, sweetheart. You know what? We're the biggest tribe of all. That's right. Us Sidewalk Indians. Hee Hee Hee. Us homeless ones, like you and me, yeah, us Sidewalk Indians."

She turned away from the old man and her beer and all of them and walked out of the seedy bar and took the bus back to her apartment building, where another welfare mother, a neighbor, was minding Corey for her.

She preferred being alone to being one of them. She had seen such awful desperation in their Indian faces. Big-city Indians. She was truly cast adrift, without people of her own, except for Corey. Just her little son and herself and not a pot to pee in, that's what one of her ex-landlords said. "You welfare bums are all alike, not a pot to pee in, and you think you own the world."

One Saturday in spring Cecelia had taken Corey to Golden Gate Park in the little infant carrier behind the seat of her bicycle. They had stopped at a meadow across the road from the fenced-in buffalo herd to eat their apples and peanut butter and jelly sandwiches. Then Cecelia sat on a bench and enjoyed the sunshine on her face and watched Corey playing in the sandpile. Such a strong, handsome child he was and, despite everything, such a happy little boy.

A man sat down on the bench and said hello and introduced himself and began a conversation, nice and easy in his friendliness. He had a southern accent. His name was Jim, and he was from Georgia. He was an attractive man, well dressed in slacks and jacket and shiny shoes, very well groomed, with shiny dark hair flecked with gray. His hair was receding just a bit. Attractive, she thought, but much older than she. An older man. Actually, he was only thirty-three.

He had been a merchant marine, he told her, and was now a ship's mechanic, having tired of the sea last year and wanting to stay put. She looked at his hands and saw that there was no grime, that the well-manicured nails were clean, with no black grease lodged underneath. She liked his soft Georgia accent. This was perhaps his most attractive feature, his sweet southern accent.

She wondered if this former merchant marine had any tattoos. He had, as it turned out, just one: a mermaid with a bare bosom on his upper left arm, but he was ashamed of it and always tried to keep it covered. She would see it only when they were in bed together, or early in the morning before he dressed. She loved to lie in his strong arms, to lie held by that mermaid-decorated arm and listen to him talk in his Georgia way. He always called her honey.

Later he would tell her that he hadn't just happened by so casually after all. He had seen her riding her bicycle as he was driving past, had turned his car around when he could and gone looking for her. He finally found her as she sat in the sunlight eating her sandwich, and he parked his car and went ambling over to meet her, hoping that she wouldn't think he was too old for her. She looked too young, he said, to be Corey's mother, and he imagined that she was a sitter or maybe a sister or aunt. She was a beautiful girl, he told her, then amended it to "Well, maybe not really beautiful, but pretty, very pretty and arresting. Beautiful to me."

Cecelia was not in love with Jim, who became her lover. There had been others over the years since Corey's birth, but she hadn't loved any of them. None of them touched her the way Bud Donahue, Corey's father, had touched her, and she did not wish to keep any one of them in her life.

But this ship's mechanic was exciting to her. He was exciting because he was thirty-three and had sailed the seven seas, had seen all of the world and had such stories to tell. She also liked the way he looked and the way he dressed, in expensive, well-tailored suits, when he took her to restaurants; he didn't look like a mechanic. He had money to spend, too. Nobody else had ever taken her out to dinner and paid forty dollars for one meal, which was half what she paid to rent her apartment for a month. He took her away for weekends, and he bought her clothes so that she could dress up when he took her out. He was kind to her. He was a skillful and considerate lover, not easily scared off, as younger men were, by her son, who was so demanding and full of bounce and energy. But he had warned her, at the beginning of their affair, "Don't go getting attached to me, now. I'm not the marrying type. I'm just passing through. That's all."

It seemed as if her men said that to her a lot. It didn't matter. They could say it all they wanted if it made them feel that they were more desirable, that women were all wanting to ensnare them, if they wanted to believe that women wanted a "commitment." It didn't matter. But two months after Jim from Georgia and she had begun their affair, he asked her to marry him.

He showed up one day and told her to come along, he had a surprise for her. She took Corey and went with him. He was smiling all the way, and he kept reaching over to touch her hand. He seemed very happy.

The surprise was a tract house in South San Francisco. It had three bedrooms and a little yard in back. He asked her if she would like to live in this house. Corey was running from room to room. Cecelia looked around, tried to imagine living here, thought of her shabby little one-room apartment. So much space here, just look at it. Jim took her in his arms. She was very used to his touch now. It felt familiar and natural after just two months.

He said, "Would you like to be married? Would you like that, honey?" He said it as if he knew that she would, that it was her most cherished dream. He explained that a friend of his was getting divorced. The friend and the soon-to-be-ex-wife wanted to sell their house. He could get a good deal. Cecelia hadn't expected this.

He was a kind man, in his way, but there were so many things about him . . . He had a large painting of the Golden Gate Bridge, done on black velvet, on his living-room wall. On the shelf by the back window of his car he had a ceramic dog with a head that wobbled when the car moved. She couldn't see herself married to him. She wanted her life to grow and become, she wanted to stretch herself and learn new things. There was so much to the world. Now she had nothing, absolutely nothing, not even a pot to pee in, and a little boy to raise all alone, and this man was offering her marriage, financial security, a house in the suburbs. There would probably be more children soon, and she could see herself driving her station wagon full of kids to the supermarket. She didn't think any of this would make her life better. But maybe it would. Maybe she wasn't really going anywhere. Maybe she was a fool for believing that her life would ever get any better. Maybe all there was in store for her, as for so many others she saw in the wretched buildings where she lived, was a life of poverty and deprivation, a life of being on welfare. This house in the suburbs and marriage to a kind man who was a good lover and provider might not be such a bad alternative. She liked the expensive restaurants and the Georgia accent and the mermaid tattoo. Jim reminded her of a child who had prepared a wonderful surprise for his mother's birthday.

When he asked her to marry him, it was as though he were offering her a tremendous prize. He had said he didn't want to get involved, fully believing that that was what she wanted, and now he was offering a commitment; she would have a husband and a house all at once. She should be overjoyed.

"I can't," she told him. "Oh, Jim, I'm so sorry, but I just can't." It hurt her to say this, to shoot him down. He had taken the chance, had made himself vulnerable, but of course, he hadn't known that it was a chance. "Thank you for asking me," she said, looking into his face. He was no longer smiling, and she couldn't read the expression in his eyes. A dark look, like a shadow, crossed his face. She had never seen him like this before. He dropped his arms, let her go. She recognized anger. A dark, awful anger.

He mocked her. "Oh, well, thank you for asking me. Sounds like I asked you to a dance or something."

They drove back to her apartment in silence. He let her off at the curb.

"I'll call you in the morning," he said, his stupid ceramic dog wobbling its stupid head in the back window as the car moved away.

Cecelia sat beside her window and smoked for a long time and watched the street below. She was a poor person. She lived in a grimy, dirty, neighborhood full of drug people and prostitutes and pimps and what-have-you, not a good environment for her child, not a good environment for her.

She was just nineteen, but sometimes she felt old. Before she met Jim, when there was no man in her life, she had felt old, as if she had no life of her own and all she lived for was to look after Corey.

After she had Nicole, she used to marvel at how calm and self-contained Nicole was, because she had imagined all young children would be like Corey, running around constantly, needing a lot of attention, seeming to want to dominate Cecelia's whole life. Once, sometime before she met Jim, she had tried to take Corey to a movie with her because she couldn't afford a sitter, but she had had to leave after fifteen minutes because he wiggled so. She grabbed him by his shoulders when they got home and screamed at him, "Do you realize you're robbing me of my youth? That's right. You are. And you know it, too! You are robbing me of my youth! You are making me a prisoner, goddammit!" And the little boy had looked at her with bewilderment in his eyes and his chin quivering and then began to cry. She held him and rocked him. "There, there, don't cry, Mommy's sorry. Mommy just got mad. She didn't mean it. Mommy's dear little boy, don't cry."

He took a long time being comforted. Afterward guilt gnawed at her: Awful person. Not fit to be a mother. You don't deserve a nice little boy. You should have given him up for adoption. Just like your mother, aren't you, picking on this helpless little child, as if it were his fault he was born.

Now at the window Cecelia knew she was tired of being the sole caretaker of her energetic young son, tired of working at low-paying jobs any moron could do and then having to go back on welfare, tired of the stigma of welfare and the rat-infested apartment buildings and budgeting her pennies, waiting for the first and the fifteenth of every month, welfare paydays, to roll around. It was no kind of life, and she could see no way out.

She sat and smoked and thought, and her thoughts went around and around in circles. She was so tired of being poor. Didn't even own a television set. She was so tired of being responsible. He wanted to take care of her. She'd felt happier with him than she had in a long, long time.

Finally, when Corey was sleeping, Cecelia went down the hallway to the pay phone, dialed the operator and placed a collect call. This was the sort of thing one would talk over with one's mother, wasn't it?

Her mother told her to marry him right away, "before he changes his mind."

"He makes good money, you say, Cecelia, and he's a good man. What is the matter with you? You don't think you can pick and choose, do you? You never were a great beauty, you know. You better marry him. You might never get asked again."

"I can't say, exactly, Mom, what the matter is. I don't love him. He doesn't, well, seem to want much from life. He doesn't read the kind of books I like to read. He doesn't read at all, in fact, except for the sports page. He isn't interested in the kind of movies I like. I don't think he's even ever been to the theater." Cecelia had been only a few times herself, mostly when she was dating an actor.

"Oh, brother," her mother said, "listen to Miss High-and-Mighty. Love, as you call it, doesn't last. *You* of all people should know that! Where is that man who probably claimed to have loved you so dearly? Where is he now, *that one*, and now here you are stuck with that innocent little boy to raise all alone?"

Her mother didn't know the story of Bud Donahue. Cecelia couldn't tell her. She couldn't risk the possibility of ridicule, of her mother spoiling her precious memories of the love she and Bud had shared.

That relationship was something she had to hold precious and secret. It was something she had to believe in, at the age of nineteen. Maybe it still was, at the age of thirty. She had to believe that their young love had been real and good and that it would have lasted, even though she knew very well that it might not have. Bud had had to believe in it, too. It was all either of them had to hang on to.

Cecelia's mother assumed that Corey's father had been some dirty lowlife who had used her and then run out on her. Cecelia's mother, after all, was worldly and experienced; she knew all about men and their wicked ways.

"And as for books and movies . . . the hell with that stuff. Books and movies, indeed. What do they matter? Not one iota. Wake up, girl. No Prince Charming is about to come along and sweep you up onto his horse. What have you got to offer a man? Think about it. Not much, do you, when you come right down to it? If you can get yourself a decent, hardworking man who will take care of you and be good to your little boy, then just thank your lucky stars."

"Thanks for the advice, Mom." Cecelia felt exhausted, but she was sure now that she had made the right decision, and she didn't need to think about it anymore. She fell into a deep, dreamless sleep.

Early the next morning she was awakened by the ringing of the telephone down the hall. She knew that it was Jim. She jumped up out of bed and ran to answer it before it woke anyone else.

"How are you this morning? Did I wake you?" He sounded friendlier now.

"No, I was already awake."

"Have you thought about what we talked about yesterday?"

"You mean about getting married?"

"Yeah. Have you thought about it?"

"I don't want to get married, Jim. I'm sorry, but I just don't want to."

"Why not?"

"I don't know. I just don't. I can't say why. But it isn't because I think there's anything wrong with you or anything, Jim. Not that."

"I know there's nothing wrong with me . . ."

"I'm sorry . . ."

"It's you. There's something wrong with you. Who the hell do you think you are? Do you think you're somebody important? You're not."

"I know I'm not. That doesn't—"

"I'll say you're not. You're nobody. I've gone with nurses and secretaries and showgirls. You don't have a damn thing going for you, do you know that? Who do you think you are, anyway, turning me down? You're just some piss-poor welfare tramp. There you are living in that ugly little hole-in-the-wall in that sleazy nigger neighborhood. You can just go straight to hell!"

She had forgotten that he always used that word "nigger" and didn't even consider it racist or rude. She was glad he had used it this last time. Along with her mother's advice, it confirmed for her that she had made the right decision.

For most of that day she stayed in bed in her nightgown and robe and pretended to nap and read a magazine, as much as she could with the boy to look after. She was moping, but trying not to look as if that was what she was doing. She wanted to mope, but she didn't want to set a bad example for Corey. Lying around and moping was not a constructive way to deal with one's problems and disappointments. And she had second thoughts.

Maybe she *was* a fool to turn that man down. Maybe she never would get another chance to marry. Her prospects certainly weren't wonderful right then. She had even applied to the Youth Opportunity Center for admission to a program in which teenage mothers could learn a marketable skill, in her case typing, while at the same time earning a high school diploma. They told her, after taking one look at her school transcripts, that she didn't have what it took to become a clerk-typist or to earn a diploma. She not only had no money but had no hopes of ever getting any.

Maybe it was all true what they said, her mother and the Youth Opportunity counselor and Jim from Georgia. Maybe she was, most unfairly, condemning her son to a lifetime of being downtrodden, of not having a pot to pee in. And why? Why couldn't she marry Jim from Georgia? It didn't make sense.

But she thought of that tract house in South San Francisco and the man who said "nigger" and had no interest in books or theater or art or lectures. She imagined a lifetime with him in that tract house, he growing paunchy and bald and sitting in front of the television watching Monday night football. No, Corey would not be better off, and they were not right about her. It might look like that now, but dammit, she was only nineteen, not even legal age. And she was better than that.

She knew that she *was* better. She was better than anyone could even guess. She deserved a good life, and somehow, one way or another, she was going to give herself one. Next year, when he was three, Corey would be old enough for the state-subsidized day-care center. She had already put him on the waiting list and said she intended to go to college at City College of San Francisco. She hadn't taken the entrance exam yet, but when she did, her scores were so good, as it turned out, that she didn't even have to take remedial English or math, as more than fifty percent of all entering freshman had to do, and most of them had graduated from high school. She wasn't sure that she would pass the exam, yet she wanted to go to college so badly, she didn't see how it could be possible that she wouldn't pass. Then she would be free; Corey would be in the center and she in college. Then she would find out what she wanted from life.

No, she didn't have to marry Jim from Georgia just to make her life easier now, because all this was only temporary, this pathetic condition she found herself in. It was just something she would have to live through, and in so doing she would develop patience and endurance. She knew with all her heart that this was true, no matter what anyone might say. She might not be able to win an argument with someone who believed she was in a trap she couldn't escape from on her own, but she knew that she could escape. Times were bad but not intolerable. She was strong enough and tough enough to live through bad times. She would show them all how good she was. They would see. Her mother would and Corey would and most of all she herself would. But not that man whose ego had just been bruised. He wouldn't ever know. He would just have to go on believing that she was a loser who had missed the chance of a lifetime.

EIGHT

Cecelia had just turned twenty-one when she entered the tuition-free City College of San Francisco. She had heard that welfare would assist mothers who enrolled at City College, but she hadn't heard exactly right. She went in to see her caseworker, Miss Wade, bringing her registration card with her and her schedule of classes, expecting that she would be given a little extra money beyond the basic $147 a month for her and Corey to live on.

Miss Wade, a thin, hunch-shouldered, middle-aged white woman in white plastic-frame glasses and bright red lipstick, sat behind her desk in the little cubicle of her office and studied the papers Cecelia had given her.

"Anthropology," Miss Wade read aloud, "English composition, Spanish, psychology." She laid the papers on the desk and took off her glasses, as if she could see better without them, and looked at Cecelia in a squinty-eyed fashion. "Are you off your rocker?" she said. "You can't handle classes like these. Anyway, what good do you think they will do you, even if you do manage to make passing grades, which I seriously doubt you could?"

"I don't know what you mean, Miss Wade. Those are required courses at all California universities."

"*Universities?* Now I've heard everything. You think you're going to a university? How absurd."

"Miss Wade, what do I have to do to get extra money to buy books and supplies now that I'm enrolled in college?"

"What *extra* money? Welfare doesn't have money to send recipients to college. Whatever gave you such a stupid idea?"

"I had a neighbor who was a welfare recipient. She went to college, and welfare paid for her books and her child care and her transportation."

"Maybe so, but she wasn't taking courses like yours, I'm sure. She was taking practical training, something to help her get a job quickly and get off the rolls and stop being a leech. Some kind of vocational training—nurse's aide, X-ray technician or dental assistant. You . . . You want the taxpayers of California to send you to college to study anthropology, for God's sake. You must be out of your mind. Do you think that's fair?"

Miss Wade slipped the white plastic-frame glasses back on, indicating that she was through talking, and pushed the registration card and schedule of classes across the surface of the desk to Cecelia.

"Why don't you just enroll yourself in a vocational program? City College has several good training programs, you know."

"Because I don't want to," Cecelia said, picking up her papers and standing. She wanted to study anthropology and psychology and Spanish because she had begun to dare to hope that maybe she could go to a university, that maybe she could get a college degree and that maybe, just maybe, she could someday study law if she was good enough.

Miss Wade shrugged. "You probably couldn't complete a vocational program, anyway," she said.

Cecelia left.

Cecelia wrote a letter to the Bureau of Indian Affairs, asking about education grants. They didn't answer. She wrote again, but this letter was also ignored. She gave up and resigned herself to the task of going to college and supporting a little boy on $147 a month. After paying rent she had $57 left, and the day-care center minimum charge was $7.00 a week, which was a bargain because they also gave Corey a hot breakfast and hot lunch. All through that first year she worried that Governor Reagan would succeed in closing down the state-subsidized day-care centers, as he had said he would, but he didn't manage to. The day-care centers survived, and she had a place to leave Corey while she was at school.

It was a hard time. She lived on the $147 from welfare her first semester at City. She couldn't buy books, so she read the texts on reserve in the library. She had to learn how to take notes and write term papers and take exams. It was a busy time, too. Sometimes all she had to eat was a bowl of cold cereal. That was all she could feed Corey, too, on those days, but he had the other meals provided by the day-care center.

She met Nathan while she was at City College. He was teaching an English class. He had recently completed his master's degree at San Francisco State and applied to a Ph.D. program at Berkeley. She thought that he was attracted to her. Once in a while she would have coffee with him or stay after class to ask his help with some of her schoolwork, but other than that she didn't think much about him.

At the beginning of the second semester she felt she couldn't hold on much longer. She went to see a counselor, because she had read an ad in the school paper: "If you are having any kind of problem, financial, emotional, academic, come to the counseling center and get help." The counselor, a cigar-smoking bald man, counseled her to quit school, get a job and save money. That was when she decided to become a criminal.

Through the work-study program she got work reading to blind students, and although it paid only a small amount of money, it made a huge difference to her. It meant she could always buy good, nourishing food. It meant she could go to a movie by herself now and then and pay a sitter. She bought herself a good pair of shoes with one of her paychecks. She did better in school, too, now that some of her money worries were lightened and she had a little more experience.

At Christmas, Cecelia took a job as a waitress at Woolworth's café in Stonestown Shopping Mall. She thought of the Christmas tree she was going to buy and the nice toys. She thought of an Oxford dictionary she wanted. As the tips added up and she was given a few overtime hours, she even began to imagine buying herself a little portable typewriter. She would need a typewriter when she transferred to Cal Berkeley, where she had by then applied for admission.

She worked two weeks at Woolworth's. Then one day Miss Wade from the welfare department came in, and it was all over. Miss Wade was worn out. She was laden with Christmas packages, and she had come into Woolworth's to relax and have a nice refreshing cup of coffee.

Cecelia didn't realize that this was Miss Wade when she set the glass of ice water down on the counter and asked if she was ready to order.

"Miss Capture, I didn't know you had a job," Miss Wade said. "Unless I am mistaken, you have not reported your earnings to our office."

Cecelia, stunned, could not speak.

"Do you know what it's called when a welfare recipient fails to report income to the department? It's called fraud, welfare fraud, and it is against the law, I'm afraid. Too bad you didn't know."

That was how she came to be a criminal, with a warrant out for her arrest. Before it was over, she ended up reporting her income from reading to blind students at City College. She knew they would check her Social Security number, anyway.

She asked them to allow her to make restitution. All told it came to $1,100. She said she would pay it all back, little by little, but they would not agree to that. They wanted to prosecute. It was a serious offense, they said, and she would have to be punished. Just paying back the money was not enough.

"I don't know how you can look at yourself in the mirror when you get up in the morning," Miss Wade said, shaking her head in disdain.

But the welfare department did not bring formal charges. Not then. Not for a while. Even though it was a misdemeanor, they could, if they wished, follow felony criminal procedure with the same penalties as those for felony. The case dragged on and on.

Months passed. Cecelia remained on the welfare rolls and continued going to City College and doing well. She was accepted at the University of California at Berkeley and awarded a scholarship.

When she moved away from San Francisco she left it all behind and did her best to forget that she had ever been a criminal. But she had only evaded justice for a time, and now she would have to pay.

_NINE

Cecelia sat on a wooden bench across from the police matron's office, waiting her turn to use the wall telephone near the south end of the hallway. She could see the daylight through a window covered with steel mesh at the end. The small area of sky she was able to see was dark and cloudy. Rain fell lightly against the windowpane.

A slender black woman in a denim jail dress held the receiver of the telephone. Looking at the floor, she said, "Yes, uh huh. Uh huh. That's right. No, I don't think so," and she nodded her head a couple of times, as if the person on the other end of the line could see her. "Uh huh. Uh huh," she said in a soft voice.

When the policewoman brought Cecelia here, Cecelia had asked if she could wait over by the window. She would have liked to stand there and look out, to see whatever might be out there, to assure herself that the outside world really existed. She was told no. Just sit and wait her turn and keep quiet. *Did she understand?* the policewoman wanted to know. *Was that clear?* Yes, she did understand, and yes, it was clear.

Was that necessary, she wondered. Did they have to treat her so rudely? Of course they didn't, but neither did they have to treat her with any courtesy, so they would, naturally, treat her like dirt. They probably treated all the prisoners badly, and there was no reason why Cecelia should be an exception. One would think, though, that they would at least allow her to shower and brush her teeth, maybe even issue her one of those little denim dresses. She felt dirty and grubby and hated feeling that way.

The woman finished her call and was taken back to her cell. The policewoman came around to Cecelia with a printed form attached to a clipboard and handed this and a pen to her. She had to sign the form before she was allowed to make her call. Cecelia couldn't help noticing that the woman's fingernails were clean and her uniform was fresh and neatly pressed. Probably she had just bathed, too. The form she was handed said that she had had the opportunity to make a phone call and had accepted. She signed her name.

"You know," the policewoman said, "we don't *have* to let you make no call." Cecelia thought of correcting her grammar but, of course, did not. "We axed you last night, and you said you didn't want to make no damn phone call. That's all we gotta give you is just one chance. We don't gotta let you change your mind once you sober up." She looked meanly into Cecelia's face, her light brown eyes shallow, flat. She had a medium-length Afro, neatly groomed, with a narrow streak of peroxided reddish orange. Something about her—her facial expression, maybe, or the tone of her voice, or the haughty manner in which she carried herself —reminded Cecelia of her sister Marie. Perhaps it was just that this woman had the upper hand and was enjoying it, was superior to Cecelia in the jail scheme of things, as Marie had been in the family scheme.

Cecelia looked down at the cement floor when she spoke, softly and politely. "Well, ma'am, I know that," Cecelia said, trying not to sound like a parody of some Step'n'fetchit character in an old movie, "and I want to thank you and let you know I sure do appreciate your letting me make this call. Awful good of you." She glanced up at the policewoman, smiling slightly, and the policewoman shrugged, handing her the dime and motioning to the pay phone with her head.

"And don't take all day, neither," the policewoman said.

"Okay. I won't," Cecelia said, trying to sound a little grateful, feeling angry and humiliated.

She dialed the operator and placed the long-distance collect call to Spokane. Corey answered the phone and accepted the call. Loud rock music blared in the background. Corey was a devoted hard-rock fan. Obviously Nathan was not at home, but she asked for him, anyway. Corey mumbled something incoherent.

"Put Nicole on, will you?" She had to shout it a second time, and this brought the policewoman out into the hallway, scowling, her hands on her hips.

"Hi, Mom." Nicole sounded happy to hear her. "When are you coming home?"

"I don't know, honey. Not real soon."

"Oh."

"Where's your daddy?"

"Oh, he's just gone to the store. He'll be back pretty soon, I think. He's real mad today. You know how come?"

"No. How come?"

"Well, maybe I'm not supposed to tell you."

"It's okay. I'm your mom. Tell me. Why is he so mad today?"

"On account of Corey," Nicole said in a small, clear voice. Clearly this was significant. Nicole paused, waiting for Cecelia to coax her to go on.

"Oh, no. What did he do now?"

"He's been getting into all kinds of trouble. All kinds. First they found a joint in his locker, but he claimed that they planted it there. Then Dad had to go see the principal. Then Dad hit Corey, almost knocked him down, and Corey took off and didn't get home until real late, and I was asleep but I woke up because Dad was hollering around so loud. I'm not sure but I think he hit Corey again. There was a lot of noise, pounding around, falling around."

"Oh, is that all then? Did they believe Corey that the joint wasn't his?"

"I don't know. He went to school the next day. That was today. He punched his math teacher and got suspended for a week.

That's how come Dad is real mad. He says maybe reform school would be a good place for Corey."

"Oh, damn. Okay, Nicole, I'll call Daddy back in a few minutes. Tell him when he gets home, okay? I don't want him to leave again."

"Okay. Mom?"

"What?"

"I wish you would come home. It's all awful without you. Sometimes I miss you so much I just lie in my bed and cry. Please come home."

"Oh, honey, I miss you, too. I'll come home as soon as I can. Just remember, I love you. Always."

"I love you, too." Cecelia could tell by the way her little girl's voice quivered that she was crying.

"Good-bye, Nicole."

"Good-bye."

Then the sound of the dial tone, an inky-black, outer-space sound. A void. Nothing.

Cecelia told the policewoman that she had tried to reach her husband but he had gone to the store, and asked permission to call again, and the policewoman agreed to allow her to make that call. Just sit down and wait, she said. Not by the window. Back on the bench. She could hear the policewoman talking and joking with some girl friend on the telephone in a low voice; she couldn't make out the conversation.

Corey always was a rambunctious child, and Nathan had become more and more irritated with him. Corey didn't do well in school, and Nathan found fault with him for that. Damn Nathan. Damn Nathan. Why was she so stupid, anyway? Why had she married such a self-centered, mean, insensitive man? How different it might have been if Corey's real father had lived. It would have been different for both of them. Then Corey would have had a father who loved him and was proud of him and wouldn't have kept putting him down all the time and calling him stupid. Then she would have had a husband who loved her. She thought of Bud Donahue and the way it had been. She was just sixteen when she met Bud.

130

*   *   *

In the last part of the summer of 1966, the year Cecelia was
sixteen, she left home, because she couldn't put up with her crazy
mother any longer and she could see no future for herself in
Wapato. If she stayed she would, probably, like the other girls she
knew, end up married to some Indian or Mexican boy and have
a lot of children. She would be poor and miserable and have to
work in the fields alongside her husband to make ends meet, and
in a short time she would be fat and tired and old. At twenty-five,
maybe. She had seen women that young already old.

Cecelia had had a hundred dollars in the bank, which she
withdrew to buy herself a Greyhound bus ticket to San Francisco,
the place where all the young people thought of running away to
when they thought of running away in 1966. "Like a thief in the
night," her mother lamented later. After all her mother had done
for her, she had stolen away in the dead of night and caught a
bus to California and wasn't heard from again for over a year.
Mary Theresa didn't know whether she was alive or dead.

In San Francisco Cecelia had found work the very day she
arrived as a waitress at the El Charro Mexican Restaurant on
Mission Street. She told them that she was not a Mexican. It
didn't matter. She had to wear a stupid Mexican peasant-girl
costume anyway: off-the-shoulder white peasant blouse and short,
gathered skirt and big gold hoop earrings. It wasn't so bad working
at El Charro. It was her first job, and she was self-supporting at
long last.

She rented a room in an old Victorian mansion on Haight
Street, where a lot of cockroaches and five cats who belonged to
nobody and ten other young people, who smoked a lot of dope,
lived. There was also Lupine. She was thirty at least, even had grey
hairs, yet she tried to act as if she was one of them, in her late
teens or early twenties. Cecelia wasn't wild about living with these
people, who were all white and had the habit of saying "Far out"
and "Can you dig it?" and "That's cool" and other such hip
things. It was new, though, and she was young and felt free and
not a bit afraid, and life was an adventure.

On her second Sunday in San Francisco, Cecelia went to a

human-be-in in the panhandle of Golden Gate Park. Janis Joplin and Big Brother, unknowns then, were playing for free. The Jefferson Airplane was a "new group from Marin; check them out." The Airplane was already gaining a reputation among the denizens of Haight-Ashbury. All those old bands, some of which became famous, most of which never left obscurity, played for free at the human-be-ins in Golden Gate Park.

It was a warm, sunshiny day. People kept giving the two-raised-fingers salute that in another time had meant "victory" but now meant "peace." All they were saying was give peace a chance. She settled down on the cool, cool green grass. It was all unbelievably pleasant. Another world. Full of color and excitement and new trends. Cecelia wore her hair long and loose, perfectly straight, and was dressed in a full-length flowing flower-print gown from India, which she had borrowed from Lupine because her own unhip small-town clothing would be sadly out of place at a be-in. It was nice of Lupine to lend it, but Cecelia noticed that the dress, although very pretty, all turquoise and light blues and greens, had that white person's underarm sweat odor, which became more apparent the warmer she became. It smelled very strong to her, but she was too involved in what was going on around her to be bothered very much. She saw a boy wearing a Viking helmet with horns sticking out at the sides, girls with long Indian-print dresses and garlands of flowers entwined in their hair; she inhaled the odor of incense and dope, which smelled like burned rope. Clangy jewelry, sandals, bare feet, dogs wearing red or blue western handkerchiefs tied around their necks running free all over the place. Peace and love. Mellow and laid back. Very California. Very Haight-Ashbury. And all they were saying was give peace a chance. The sun felt good. The music sounded good. She had a job and a place to stay. Nobody hassled her anymore. Everything was just fine.

Cecelia noticed a young man milling about in the crowd. He didn't seem to belong. He was tall and well built and had nice shoulders and a firm, flat stomach. At the age of thirty, she could still remember clearly how the sight of that strange young man had touched her, how beautiful she thought he was. But he seemed out of place at the Haight-Ashbury be-in.

First, it was his hair, dark and curly. It was much, much too short for this time and place. It could have been a great head of hair, a great, woolly, bushy tumbleweed of a head of hair. She wondered why he kept his hair so short.

There were many, many people there, and the music was loud, and there was a woman dressed up to look like death personified, in a hooded dark robe, carrying a scythe, telling everyone that she symbolized death and Vietnam. She also carried a lighted black candle. Her face was white except for the hollows of her cheeks and the hollows of her eyes, which were painted black. The odor of marijuana and incense hung heavily in the air.

It began to not feel quite so mellow all of a sudden. Not all of the people were young. Some were dressed in hippie costumes, but they didn't quite make it, didn't quite pull it off. Dope dealers. A lot of dope dealing was going on, on the sidelines— Owsley Acid, reds, uppers and downers, speed. Speed, man, yeah. Methadrine, crystal. Janis sang the blues while the dope was dealt.

Bad-news speed freaks and other kinds of freaks with pimples walked around talking to themselves with bad teeth in their weird-looking heads. Dope dealers. Still Janis sang the blues, and mellowed-out people danced on the grass.

That young man, where was he? What else made him seem out of place? What else besides the short hair? It was his expression. There was a certain intensity about him, a worried, pensive look.

Someone handed her a joint. She knew what it was, of course, her house being a suburb of Dope City and all. But she didn't like it. It burned her throat and made her eyes sting. She didn't like its effects, either. Some especially hip kids back in Wapato smoked dope. Weed. Grass. But not many. The people at the place where she lived smoked it. Who were they? Rainbow and Eastern Star, a guy named Rabbi who didn't look at all Jewish, and someone from Argentina. She never really smoked dope, just took a toke now and then when they insisted. She had learned to pretend and got out of it gracefully most of the time.

She took a long toke now and passed it on. It seemed fitting somehow to smoke dope here. She held the smoke in her lungs for a long time. It made her feel light-headed. She started thinking about Wapato and her parents. She felt so sorry for them all. They were so pitifully unaware. She began thinking of her poor, crazy mother and her miserable life, and she felt almost like crying. Were they worried about her? She should have left them some kind of note, but she didn't want them to know where she was going. They might try to track her down.

Her mother was always telling her that her sisters had all been married by the time they reached her age, so obviously she considered sixteen a grown-up age. Then they shouldn't worry, and they probably didn't, and she would stop thinking about them.

Cecelia was glad she wasn't in Wapato anymore. She was glad she had come to San Francisco. It was a magic place to her, all white and beautiful, rising up out of the bay. When she first saw San Francisco, she knew that it was where she was meant to be. But she didn't like it so much anymore. It was the dope. It made her feel tense and uncomfortable.

Then the curly-haired young man was at her side. He was smiling at her. Oh, but he *was* an attractive young man. Like a garden. So nicely arranged, so fresh and alive. She wanted to touch him . . . so she did. She reached out and rested her hand on his bare arm. He smiled. It was the dope distorting her personality. She didn't go around touching strange guys in the park. She smiled back at him. She loved him. She was filled with love for him; she felt warm and friendly and erotic.

He asked her her name. She wished she had an exotic name, like Rainbow. Or Lorelei. Or Sunshine. But she didn't. Her name was just plain old Cecelia. She said her name to him, and he repeated it twice, "Cecelia. Cecelia. Beautiful name. Beautiful girl." He touched her hair, touched her face. Tenderly.

"Are you Indian, Cecelia? You look like maybe you are."

She had to laugh. He couldn't tell for sure. He had to ask. How funny it was. He was a white guy, and he thought her being Indian was neat and exotic. Yes, she told him. Certainly. He laughed, too.

A long-haired hippie at her other side passed her another joint. A very skinny guy, no doubt into dieting. Those people liked to be as thin as possible. His arms looked like broomhandles. "Love, sister, peace," he said and embraced her. "Beautiful." His long hair was thin and stringy, tied down with a piece of leather lace knotted behind his head. His big ears stuck out through his thin brown hair.

Cecelia passed the joint. The curly-haired young man told her that his name was Bud. No, it wasn't, it was really Brian. But they had called him Bud from the time he was a little boy. Bud. Brian. She loved being near this man.

If only she had known then that he was going to be her son's father and that she wouldn't have long to look at him, she would have studied his face and tried very hard to memorize everything about him.

After the third toke, she didn't like it at the be-in anymore. She felt alone and afraid. As if they were all out to get her. She saw dirty, unkempt people. She thought of lice. They all seemed threatening to her now, a moving, churning sea of humanity. There were too many of them. It was Chaos. No order at all, not anywhere, not in anything. Even the music was disorderly. She could no longer feel any good vibes of love and brotherhood.

She was offered another joint but shook her head.

"Whatsmatter? Are you uptight or somethin'? Hey, man, what are you, a narc or somethin'?"

"Narc?"

"Narc? Who? Where? Who said narc?"

The very word "narc" was enough to send paranoid vibes through the crowd. She took a fourth toke, for the sake of not being thought a narc, and passed it on.

Bud put his arm around her, a nice strong, protective arm. She hid her face in his shoulder. He felt so right. It seemed to her he was what she had been missing all her life. The other part of herself. He held her, encircled her in his arms, stroked her hair.

"Beautiful hair," he whispered, "beautiful."

By the time night had fallen, Cecelia and Bud were at her place over on Haight. She had thought that the walk in the night air would help to clear her head, would detoxify her somewhat, but the influence of the grass was still there, and she hated it and wanted it to be gone. She could not remember ever feeling so afraid. It was worse than fear, almost panic, and there was no specific cause. It was as if someone was out to get her and was not too far behind. It was as if some terrible impending doom was lurking in the shadows. She could barely speak. Her tongue felt thick and awkward. Everything was in slow motion.

She and Bud sat down on the mattress that served as a divan in the living room. The place was full of people, most of whom she didn't know. They were smoking dope, jumping rope, reading Ferlinghetti, eating spaghetti, talking about karma and reincarnation and what was going on with Dylan and, of course, the topic nobody ever quit talking about, Vietnam.

There was Ravi Shankar music. It sounded like water. It sounded peaceful. She would sure like to be in the place that the music described. Rainbow asked them if they wanted some spaghetti. Bud ate. Cecelia took a beer from the refrigerator.

Although she had tried to drink beer several times before, she had never liked it much. It was too bitter and too strong, and it always got warm before she managed to polish off an entire bottle. This time she did like it. She loved it, in fact. Her mouth was parched, and the beer was ice-cold and refreshing, like those beer commercials from The Land of Sky Blue Waters, the bottles of beer, all amber and frosty, sitting in the middle of the rapids, held in place by white rocks.

Bud came over to her and embraced her, nuzzled her neck and said, "Hey, what do you want to do now, kid?"

"Have another beer," she said, and he did, and she did, too, and it made her feel a little more relaxed, but she still felt some vague threat she could not quite understand, as if reality wasn't the way it seemed, wasn't the way the people in the house were trying to make it appear—Rainbow and her old man and the one she didn't like whose dress she was wearing, the one who seemed to be too old to be hanging around with a bunch of kids like them, Lupine. What a strange name. Probably made up, but didn't Lupine have something to do with wolves? Wasn't that what the name meant? Yes. Wolves. Werewolves to be exact. Creepy old Lupine.

How did that old saying go about wolfsbane, which werewolves were said to be partial to? "Even a man who is pure of heart . . ." How did it go? No matter. Lupine was probably just a sad, overaged hippie. *Maybe* that's all she was. If Cecelia was lucky, that was all she was.

Maybe Rainbow and Lupine and What's-his-name, Rainbow's old man, were all involved in some kind of conspiracy against her. And, Christ Almighty, they were white, weren't they? All of them. White and hairy as could be. White, white, white. Sickly white like the underbellies of frogs or certain kinds of fish. She had to try to stop seeing them as white. She had somehow to shift gears. She opened up another bottle of beer and chugalugged half of it down. That was better, much better.

Brian was the only one she trusted. The only one here. The only one anywhere. He was her man. He transcended his whiteness somehow. She didn't know how. It didn't matter. To her he was all that was safe and good and stable, and she trusted him absolutely, would have trusted him with her very life. He was like a frontier marshall, like Matt Dillon in Dodge City, come to make things safe again for decent folks like herself. His body was so strong, and look at the lines of his face, the clean, beautiful bone structure, chiseled features. Handsome boy.

She was looking at his face, admiring him, loving being with him, when he took the half-full bottle of beer from her hand, set it on the table, gathered her in his arms, kissed her full on the mouth and asked again, "Baby, what would you like to do now, really?"

She said, without thinking, "I want you to come to my room with me. I want you to lie down beside me. I want us to hold each other."

That was really what she meant. Just that. He smiled. They went to her room, and he undressed her first and then himself, kissing her and touching her as he went along. And then they pulled back the covers and got into bed together.

She went into his arms so naturally it was as if she had known him a long, long time and getting into bed together was something they always did. It didn't seem at all strange, and Bud didn't ask her if he could, the way the boys back home would ask, "Please let me, please, I'll be careful," he just did, and she forgot the part about being a virgin that had to be gotten out of the way first.

She had to tell him because there was the physical resistance when he attempted to penetrate her. He asked her what the matter was, why was it so difficult? Did she have a hang-up or something? He seemed bewildered. Did she not want him after all? She guessed he had never been with a virgin before. So she had to explain to him. She hoped he wouldn't be disappointed, that he wouldn't think she wasn't a grown woman after all, or too inexperienced for him, but it was all right.

He was pleased, very pleased that he was the first one, and he took great care, and it hurt only a little, and then it was possible for him to be close to her truly, for her to be close to him, closer than she had ever been to any person, so close, so close that she shut her eyes and touched him as he was touching her and lost all track of him and herself, where one began and the other ended, and they were not separate anymore.

All night long it went on. Sometime toward morning he told her that his real name was Brian. He had said that before, but he forgot that he had. This was important, he said. He wanted her to listen carefully and remember. His last name was Donahue. He was born and raised in a suburban community not far from Berkeley, just across the bay, called El Sobrante. Now he had something very important to tell her. He held her tightly to him, and she rested her face against his chest. He smoothed her hair, kept stroking her hair. It was hard to tell her this, he said. He was a soldier. He was going to ship out in just a few days for Da Nang.

"Are you afraid?" she asked him. She was afraid for him. She didn't want him to go. He could do something, couldn't he? He didn't have to go just because they said he had to. But, yes, he *did* have to go, and yes, he was afraid. He was trying not to be but he was, yes, he was afraid.

Later on they went to a little café on Haight Street and ate pancakes and drank orange juice and looked at each other and touched hands under the table. They went home again and showered together and then went back to bed and made love again and slept in each other's arms and woke up and made love again.

Bud told her he needed her. It pleased him that he was the first man to make love to her. He loved her, he said. Nobody had ever said they loved and needed her before.

She loved him. With all her heart and soul. All of the love that she had locked inside her with no one to give it to was his now, and she gave it with much pleasure. She would be his forever, she told him, forever, and always.

The next day she called in sick at her new job so that she could spend the time with him. Every minute of their time together was precious. But it was all over quickly, so very quickly.

Just three days and nights of love, and then he was gone.

He wrote one letter, which she answered immediately. She never heard from him again. She knew that he had either been killed or badly wounded or was a prisoner of war. She knew that he wouldn't just not write her. But she couldn't accept the alternatives. He was only nineteen, and he didn't even know that he was going to be a father, and besides, dammit, he was hers, he belonged to her! It was monstrously unfair.

In that one letter he wrote that thinking of her was the only thing that made it bearable, it was all so awful and ugly. He would die, he wrote, if he didn't have their time together to remember, if he didn't have her to think about going home to. The letter ended: "Think of me very hard every night, and I will think of you."

She did think of him, too, even though, try as she might, she could not remember his features clearly. What she could remember was how it felt to be held in his arms and how good it was to tell someone that she loved him, someone who would say the same thing to her. She remembered those feelings and a vague picture of a good-looking curly-haired young man. He was smiling in the pictures she had of him in her mind.

She thought of him very hard as she waited tables at El Charro in her silly little Chiquita peasant-girl outfit, aware, too aware, that her breasts were swollen and tender and that her period was very late.

In her sixth month of pregnancy she entered a home for unwed mothers in San Francisco. She was given faded, threadbare maternity clothes that looked as if they had been cut out of printed flour sacks. They all had that pungent white woman's underarm odor, every maternity smock in the place. Her first week there she called the Donahues in El Sobrante, who confirmed what she had already known without acknowledging it to herself, that Bud had been killed in Vietnam, right after he had written that first letter. She had known it but had still hoped it wasn't true. The Donahues came the next day to see her. They were young people, in their early forties.

"It's like a miracle," Mrs. Donahue said, dabbing at tear-filled eyes. "A miracle." She hugged Cecelia warmly. Their only child was dead, but they were going to be grandparents. They gave her a photograph of Bud, which she kept along with the letter Bud had written her, until she married Nathan. Bud was a young boy in the photograph. It was his high school graduation picture in a gold-colored metal frame.

Cecelia was just seventeen when Corey Donahue was born. She immediately went downtown and got on Aid to Families with Dependent Children and moved to a shabby furnished one-room apartment in the Western Addition.

Corey's paternal grandparents helped out some, but not much. They would bring over a box of groceries once a month, more often if she asked them, which she did only a time or two. Sometimes Grandpa Donahue would slip her a twenty-dollar bill and caution her not to mention this to Grandma.

The Donahues took Corey for weekend visits. They wanted to keep him permanently. They said to Cecelia, "You're so young, Cecelia. Why not let us take Corey, and you go on with your young life. It isn't good for you to be so tied down, and it isn't good for your little boy to have to live the way the two of you must. He would be better off with us in El Sobrante." But Cecelia would not allow them or anyone to take him away from her. Corey was her son, she told them, not theirs. He was not some unwanted, thrown-away remains of an abortion. He was not the product of some desperate, destitute, unwed teenage mother given up for adoption. He was *her son*. She would take care of him and raise him, watch him grow into a man. Someday she herself would be a grandmother. Someday she would have a bigger family, and that was something she looked forward to. But for then, when she was seventeen, it was just the two of them, just Cecelia and Corey, her own beautiful, perfect baby boy.

The Donahues were fond of telling her that Corey was "the spitting image" of his father, and maybe he was. He showed his Indian blood only a little. His complexion was nearly as dark as his mother's, but he always spent a lot of time in the sun, and while his hair was black, it was curly, like Bud's had been, and his eyes were green, sometimes greyish. Maybe he looked like a Harrigan, as Mary Theresa claimed he did.

At the age of thirteen, Corey was even more like Bud. He was a tall, husky Irishman, nothing like his stepfather, Nathan, who was blond and slender. Poor Corey, who tried so hard, had never done well in school. Bud wouldn't have berated him for that. Now Corey was playing hooky and getting caught with joints in his school locker and, worst of all, had hit a teacher and got himself suspended. Where were they all headed? What was going to become of them?

Cecelia could see through the window at the end of the hall that the sky was darker and the rain was harder. It hit against the windowpane in little thuds. She longed to go look out, just once, just to look down and see the street. She knew there would be no use in asking, though.

She asked the black policewoman, who reminded her of her sister, if she could try to call her husband again, and she was granted permission.

This time Nathan was the one who answered the phone.

"Nathan, I'm in jail. They arrested me for drunken driving and now they're keeping me on an old warrant for welfare fraud."

"Welfare fraud? When did that happen?"

"A long time ago, Nathan. Years ago, when I was on welfare."

"Are you guilty? Did you really do it?"

"Yes, I did, and they aren't going to let me out unless you come down and get me out. The bond has been set at twenty-five thousand dollars. You can't do it by mail. You'll have to come down and get me out, or I'll have to stay here."

"That might not be such a bad idea, to let you sit down there in jail. You're just like your hooligan son. Lies and deceit and cheating and fraud. That is just so like you, Cecelia. Why did you do it? Why on earth did you do it? Lots of people survive on welfare without having to cheat. I never did understand why it was you happened to be on welfare in the first place. Just no pride, that's all. Just lazy and worthless. You were young and able-bodied. There was no reason . . ."

"Shut up, you fucking Boy Scout!" she shouted into the receiver and slammed it down into its cradle.

The policewoman took her back to her cell without a word. Cecelia was so angry she wanted to hit or kick something, but there was nothing but the cement walls, no pillow even. She hit the thin mattress with her fist. Fucking Boy Scout! She hit it again and again: Fucking Boy Scout.

___Ten

Cecelia hated Nathan now. He didn't understand or want to understand her. His face was permanently drawn up in a frown, an attitude of disapproval, maybe even disgust, when it came to her. Yet she didn't always hate the self-righteous Nathan Welles. Once she had admired him because he was so learned, so very intelligent and cultured. She was grateful to him for the affection and comfort he had given her after her father's death. Maybe she had even loved him. She could remember believing that she did. She supposed she must in some way have loved him.

It seemed odd to her now, as she sat alone and grubby in her jail cell, her rage at Nathan spent in beating the mattress, that she had once felt that being married to him would make her happy, was in fact the only thing that *could* make her happy. She wondered what had made being married to him seem so desirable.

She was just twenty-one when she began the affair with him. She was all alone except for Corey. She was afraid and self-doubting, needy beyond words. Her father's death and the subsequent visit with her mother and sisters had left her spirit in ruins.

Every year since Corey's birth, Cecelia had taken her son home to Wapato for a day or two or three to visit her parents. Every year it was the same: Her mother grew more bitter and hateful as the years passed; her father was almost always drunk. They were both getting old. Her mother, confined to a wheelchair now, was having treatments for arthritis, but they did not seem to be making her any better. Her hands were so badly deformed that there was little she could do with them.

Each year when Cecelia left, when she returned to her own life in California, her mother's words—always the same words—echoed in her mind: "I had six children. Two of them died. I have grown daughters. Four of them, but now they are all too busy to concern themselves about me. I should have been too busy to care for them and change their dirty diapers when they were small. How foolish I was to have imagined that they would ever be a comfort to me in my old age."

And Cecelia would carry away images of her father, an old, stoop-shouldered, white-haired man coming home drunk late at night.

Her mother wrote her a letter while she was still a student at City College, before she went to Berkeley, after she had been exposed as a welfare fraud and lived every day in dreadful anticipation of how that case was going to turn out. She didn't want to go back to Wapato. She didn't want to carry the burden of her parents with her anymore. She was tired. The letter from her mother told her that the Wapato police had brought her father home. They had found him lying unconscious in an alley beside his favorite tavern. He had been badly beaten, had a broken rib, a split lip and a bloody, battered face. His billfold had been taken, but he still wore his old gold watch, the watch his father had given him when he graduated from Jesuit High School.

Another time, her mother wrote, two young men brought him home drunk as a skunk. That was at a time when the one taxi in Wapato was not operating for some reason. The two young men demanded the gold watch as payment. They said he had promised them that if they drove him home, made sure he got home safely, he would give them the gold watch. He had no money.

It would have been so easy for them to take the watch from Will's wrist, she wrote, as he sat there limply, his head hanging down on his chest, lolling to one side. The two old people lived alone in the house. Mary Theresa was so helpless, with her crippled legs and twisted hands, that she was barely able to push herself around in a wheelchair.

"No. Not the watch," Mary Theresa told the young men. "I'll get you some money. I don't have any money in the house, but I'll make a call and I'll borrow some. You cannot have that watch."

Mary Theresa tried to call Andrea, who lived just seven miles away in Yakima. No answer. She let the phone ring and ring. Still no answer.

"Hey, we want the watch, lady," one of them said. "We can't wait around here all night."

Mary Theresa finally called her next-door neighbor, a gossipy old widow, and asked to borrow ten dollars because an emergency had come up and they didn't happen to have any cash right then.

The widow next door brought over a ten-dollar bill. "My dear God," Mary Theresa wrote. "That woman saw your father sitting there slumped in his drunken stupor. Some emergency! What she must think of us now!"

The two young men took the ten-dollar bill and left. Mary Theresa worried that they might come back some day, because she had often read in the newspapers or heard on the radio news stories about vulnerable old people who lived by themselves being beaten, sometimes beaten to death—old people's bodies become so frail—and then robbed of all their money and valuables.

But much worse, to Mary Theresa, than the thought of the two strange, arrogant, threatening young men returning was the utter humiliation she had suffered in front of the widow next door.

"I should have let those hooligans take the damned old watch," she wrote to Cecelia. "Why not? It doesn't mean a damned thing to me. Now that old busybody, I'm sure, has spread it all around town. I know we must be a laughingstock: the two old fools of Wasco Avenue, a drunken fool and his crippled fool of a wife."

Reading that letter had made Cecelia dread her visit home even more. She remembered how images of her parents would repeat themselves over and over like a broken record in her mind as she went about her usual activities. She sometimes lay in her bed at night and remembered the awful things that had happened during her visits home. It was too much, she decided.

She had the welfare fraud case hanging over her head. She had been accepted at Cal Berkeley, and she knew that Berkeley would be formidable. It wouldn't be easy for her to go there and fit right in and begin competing with the whites and the middle class. She didn't feel up to seeing her parents that year and having them load her down with guilt and pain. What she needed was a little rest between the end of the City College fall semester and the beginning of the Cal Berkeley spring quarter, a period of about a month. She wrote to her mother and told her. Her mother wrote back that Cecelia thought only of herself, wanted only to cause heartache. "We aren't going to live forever," her mother wrote. "We will be gone and out of your hair soon once and for all. It seems to me like you could humor us in the few years we have left." Cecelia was glad that she had decided not to go home that year. It was during the time she would have been there that her father died.

Cecelia and Corey had been out late the night she learned of her father's death. They had gone to the zoo and then to the home of a young married couple she had made friends with at City College. They ate dinner there and all watched *Star Trek* on TV and stayed up late talking. She and Corey were both very tired by the time they got home. Corey fell asleep immediately. Cecelia was in her pajamas when she heard a knock at her door.

She opened the door, keeping the chain lock in place. It was the building manager, the old woman Cecelia had seen up close only when she first moved in; she always sent a man around to collect the rent. Once or twice Cecelia had seen her walking from her car to the apartment building or vice versa. Cecelia was surprised to find her standing at her door. She had a very serious look on her face. Cecelia couldn't imagine what the problem might be.

"May I come in, dear?" the old woman asked.

"Oh, yes, of course, excuse me, please come in."

It was cold that night, she remembered.

"Your mother called from Washington," the old woman said once she was inside the apartment. So what? Of course, if she had called, it would have to have been from Washington. Where else would her mother call from? Rio de Janeiro? What was this all about, anyway, and why was the old lady looking at her in that funny way?

"Your mother had some bad news for you, dear."

"Oh? What happened?"

"Oh, honey, I'm sorry. This is something that everyone has to live through, that is, if they live long enough. It's just another part of life. I was only a child when I lost my father."

She was only a child? Why was it always so hard to imagine old people as children? They had been children once, of course, yet it always seemed strange when they said "when I was a child."

The old woman kept looking at her with unbearable sympathy in her watery blue eyes. Cecelia felt a chill move down her back. She wished she could stop this old woman for just a couple of heartbeats. She needed more time. Stop. Please don't go on. Not yet.

It was quiet inside her apartment. Not much traffic on this street, and the bus had quit running. Not much activity. Where were all the hustle-and-bustle noises a big city is always supposed to have? All she could hear was the loud hum of the old fridge and the crashing roar of the ocean, which was not close enough to be a roar but more like a rumble. A faraway rumble in her ears. But she knew that the ocean was really too far away for her to hear. The rumble was inside herself.

And she was aware of the strong odor of . . . what, what was it? Lilacs. The old woman was wearing lilac cologne. Cecelia's mother loved lilacs. She wondered why the old woman bothered with lilac cologne. She hardly ever ventured outside her apartment, just stuck around in there with her five cats. Did the cats appreciate the lilac cologne?

"Dear," the old woman said, "do you understand what I'm trying to tell you?"

She had caught her breath. It was all right now. She could move forward again.

"My father," she said, like a schoolgirl called upon to recite, "my father is dead."

The old woman said that she was sorry.

"Oh, it's all over now. He's dead," Cecelia said aloud, but more to herself than to the old woman. "I guess I should pack, then. I have to make arrangements. Try to borrow some money for the trip. Thank you. Thank you very much." She could not remember the old woman's name. She made her rent checks out to Granada Realty.

When the old woman had gone, Cecelia thought about what she had just heard. Dead. He wasn't dead. This was just another one of her mother's tricks to get her to come home. That was all it was.

Well, okay, she would go along with it. She would go on up there and see for herself, and her mother would be glad to see her, and so would her father. He would be sitting out in the back with his reading glasses on, and he would be filing his saws. No, it would be too cold up there for that. He would be in the garage probably, working on his car. His big hands would be all black and greasy.

Her parents would have a special dinner to celebrate her home-coming: pork chops and mashed potatoes, their favorites.

Her mother, if confronted, would pretend that the old woman at the Granada Apartments had "gotten her wires crossed," and she would laugh it off. She would not admit to the trick. That was the way her mother was, sneaky and never admitting her own sneakiness.

Cecelia knew, of course, that all this was nonsense. She knew that her father was really dead.

She turned on the radio, switched it to AM, away from the FM classical station she usually listened to in an effort to become more cultured. She dialed KCOW, the Bay Area's good old down-home country and western music station.

Her spirits lifted some as the country and western twanged on. Good ole George Jones and Tammy Wynette. Good ole Hank Williams Junior and Conway Twitty. That kind of music made her think of Wapato, back on the reservation, when she was a young girl growing up.

She brought out her suitcase and all the cardboard cartons and began packing. She packed clothes, dishes, books, toys. It would all have to go, have to be stored somewhere while she was away, because when she came back she would not be returning to this shabby little apartment in Western Addition. She would never again live in the slums. When she came back she would be moving into a clean, efficient, boxy apartment in student family housing in Berkeley, and the rent would be the same as she paid for the little hole-in-the-wall. It would be nice. She was going to buy Corey a tricycle, and he would have a nice, safe place to ride it in the courtyard of their new apartment complex. Life was going to be better for the two of them from then on.

As she packed, she thought of Wapato, and she could visualize the Valley, the orchards, the fields of mint and sugar beet and hops. Everything grew in the Yakima Valley. Well, not everything, not oranges and pineapples, not tropical fruit. But everything else. She remembered the vineyards and the smell of the sugar-beet refinery and the odor of mint in the air. She could visualize the mountains.

She thought of all her old friends. Her old six-pack, the teenage girls she used to run with, just before she went away to California. She remembered the time she dressed up in high-heeled shoes and a sophisticated, pinned-up hairdo and makeup and tried to buy a case of beer for the six of them when they went swimming down at the river. They had gone to several places, and it didn't look as if it was going to work, but finally she went into a tavern. The tavern was very dark, and the bartender was engrossed in watching the World Series. He didn't even look at her as he brought her the case of beer, took her money, made change. His eyes were glued to the TV the whole time. When she came out of the tavern, her friends jumped up and down. She had done it! She scored a case of beer!

They used to go everywhere together, until they got older and began spending some of their time with boys. Oh, those were fine

Wapato summers, long hot summers. Movies and swimming in the river. They often had a little money because of the field work that was available. Summer was the time of the White Swan All-Indian Rodeo and celebration. There were always a lot of interesting guys at White Swan. Guys from Calgary, Alberta, Wyoming and Montana, cowguys in fancy embroidered western shirts and Stetson hats showing off for the local Yakima Valley girls.

She remembered White Swan and the gambling and the exhibition dancing, war dancing, bear dancing, social Indian dancing, done mostly by older people. She could hear the drumbeat and the singing of the songs. She missed Wapato.

She thought that it would feel good to be back home in the Valley again.

By daybreak she had finished her packing and was sitting in the big chair smoking, pensive, trying to keep herself steady and not think of anything.

Corey got up earlier than usual, rubbing his eyes.

"Hi, Mom," he said.

"Hi, Son. Come here a minute. I want to tell you something."

He came to her, and she hugged his warm little body. He was dressed in his blue pastel pajamas with feet. He was getting too big to wear that kind of sleepwear. This would probably be his last pair of pajamas with feet.

"How would you like to go stay in El Sobrante for a while?"

"Oh, wow! El Sobrante! Neato. How come?"

"I've got to go away for a few days. My dad died."

"Who died? You mean Grandpa Capture?"

"Yeah. Grandpa Capture."

"Who killed him? Does Grandpa Capture got blood all over him?"

"I don't know everything about it yet, Corey. I've got to call my mom. But he was very old, you know. I think he probably just got too tired to go on living anymore." She hoped that he hadn't been beaten to death by some young thugs or anything like that. She hoped it was the way she had told Corey that it probably was.

"Oh," Corey said, nodding his head. "When are you going?"

"Today. That is, if I can get it all together today."

Corey went to fix himself a bowl of raisin bran. When he poured the milk, he lost control, and the milk spilled onto the table. He looked at his mother in alarm.

"I'll clean it up, Mom," he said.

She watched the milk spread across the table, drip onto the floor.

"Get the sponge, Corey," she said and he did. The twangy country music droned on. Monotonous. All country songs sounded alike after a while. Corey finished wiping up the mess and began to eat his cereal. Cecelia would have to do it over again because he didn't get all of it. She switched the radio off. There. The quiet was better. She sat still in the big chair. She felt weary now as she anticipated the long day ahead of her.

She had forgotten how much it cost to telephone to El Sobrante. She would have to call the Donahues collect and ask to borrow money for the trip home and ask them to take care of Corey for her.

ELEVEN

Afterward, when her sisters had all gone and she was alone in the house with her mother, Cecelia tried to recall the wake and the funeral because she wanted to organize it all into a coherent package in her own mind. But she found she had no really clear memories. She wished she had someone back in California whom she could tell what had happened, but there was no one. If she had to deliver an account of it, it might make it easier for her to understand. She tried to imagine an account.

She had begun to feel small on the bus on the way to the San Francisco airport, and she kept on getting smaller and younger until, when her plane landed at the Yakima airport, she felt like a defenseless child again.

She had come to Washington without either a car or a coat, and this would make her more dependent on her mother and sisters than she had been since she really was a child, for the funeral was not to take place in Wapato. The body was going to be transported back to Northern Idaho, where it was still winter, for burial in the tribal cemetery. She had not owned a coat or any warm clothes since she moved to California. She borrowed a coat from a teenage niece, who agreed to the loan very reluctantly and acted as if she hated both lending it and the person who borrowed it.

Cecelia never cried, not when she heard the news, not when she saw him lying dead in his casket at the wake, not when they lowered the wooden coffin into the grave in the frozen, black Idaho earth. She just thought how she had imagined him visiting her at Cal Berkeley someday. She would give him a tour of the campus, and he would especially love the view from the campanella. He would be proud of her, and he would be in awe of the big, prestigious university. She had never told him that she planned to study law. She was going to wait until she had successfully completed an academic year at Berkeley. She would tell him then, and he would be proud and happy. Now it would never be. He was dead.

Her mother told her how awful she looked, like a California hippie with that stringy long hair (her mother had always hated her hair) and black tights. And her sisters ridiculed her speech, mocked what they said was her "fake California accent." Strange that no one else ever thought she had an odd way of speaking.

Her mother and her sisters all shed many tears at the wake and the funeral. Cecelia felt very little of anything, except the cold. What passed for cold in California was not like this. She had been away so long she had forgotten what real cold was, how the wind blistered your face and whipped your legs even if they were covered with hippie tights. The priest hadn't known Will Capture, but he did know that he was not much of a churchgoer. He preached a sermon about how some people didn't bother going to church except when they needed something, like being buried. It was almost funny. The whole thing had an unreal quality about it, except for the cold. Nothing meant anything. Cecelia felt numb.

The wake was held at the tribal community center and lasted only one night. When Cecelia was a little girl, wakes were held in the dead person's home and lasted three days and nights. After the burial everyone returned to the home of the deceased for a feast and giveaway. Now it was at the tribal community hall and lasted just one night.

Cecelia and Andrea and a few people who had been close friends and relatives of Will Capture stayed with the body all night, keeping a vigil. The other sisters and Mary Theresa went to motels in town and returned in the morning.

The niece who had lent Cecelia the coat took it back and nearly left with it, but one of the other nieces told Cecelia this was happening. She looked across the wide hall and saw her niece on the other side, with her mother, Marie, and they were walking fast. The niece was carrying the navy-blue wool coat over her arm. Cecelia had to call to them and run to catch up.

They stood near the door looking mean and angry, one very much like the other, a mother-daughter team, as Mary Theresa and Marie were a mother-daughter team.

"Are you leaving with the coat?" Cecelia asked. "Did you forget you lent it to me? Do you know it's ten degrees outside tonight?"

The mother-daughter team didn't speak at first. The daughter clutched the coat closer for a moment in a protective, possessive gesture. The mother-daughter team looked at each other; then the daughter spoke. "Oh, all right. Here, take it," and as Cecelia took the coat, the niece, who was seventeen, said, "I took it because you threw it over a chair where the kids were playing. They could have knocked it to the floor and stepped on it. This time you take better care of it!" And the mother-daughter team gave Cecelia a hard, icy look, their already small eyes narrowed to slits. Twerps, Cecelia thought. They were all a bunch of twerps, her family. It didn't matter, though, any of it. She would be back in California soon, a long way from them. What mattered right now was that she have a coat to keep herself warm.

When it was all over and Cecelia was back in Wapato with her mother, she continued to feel unreal. Her mother seemed even sillier than she used to be. She read books by Edgar Cayce and Jeane Dixon, and she subscribed to *Fate* magazine. Sometimes she would call Catherine or Marie long-distance, and since Cecelia was in the same room, she couldn't help but hear her mother telling them that she was just calling to say hello because she was so lonely and miserable and had no one to talk to.

Mary Theresa would go on to say she supposed she would have to go into a nursing home now that she was old and sick and helpless, since none of her beautiful daughters cared enough about her to care for her as she had cared for them, changing their shitty diapers and nursing them and all of that. The others at least had big families to take care of and jobs. Cecelia had nothing. She had only Corey, and the two of them could easily live in the house on Wasco Avenue with Mary Theresa. No, they could not, Cecelia thought when she heard her mother saying that. She would die before she would go back to Wapato and spend her life taking care of her mean, crazy old mother.

Sometimes, in the days following her father's burial, Cecelia would sit in Will Capture's old chair and stare out the window at the new tree stump. The stump, of course, reminded her and her mother and all who looked at it that her father had died of a heart attack after cutting that tree down and chopping it into logs.

"I told him not to do it," Mary Theresa said, as if trying to absolve herself of her husband's death, as if someone held her responsible. "I told him not to do it. A man his age. He wouldn't listen to me. He never did. He had to saw that tree down. It was an obsession. It was on account of Schultz next door. You remember old Schultz, don't you?"

Of course she remembered Mr. Schultz, and she remembered the tree, too. She had always liked that tree. She thought it the most attractive feature of Wasco Avenue, and whenever she thought of Wapato, she thought of it.

It was a kind of tree Cecelia wasn't familiar with, a kind that did not grow in their old home in Idaho. It was very old and very big, and its trunk was thick. It rose high, and its branches spread wide all around in intricate little twists and turns, stretching, reaching beyond itself, outward and skyward.

In winter, the tree's branches were leafless and exposed and looked dark and dramatic against the cold sky, or strange and ethereal when they were covered with delicate crystal ice, sparkling on dull days, dazzling in the bright winter sun. In summer, though, the branches weren't visible, just the trunk below and the heavy green foliage. The tree provided a great deal of shade, and not just for the Capture yard. The branches reached out over the next-door neighbor's yard, too, and provided him with the same deep shade, though it was Will Capture who pruned and watered and otherwise cared for the tree.

The neighbor was a skinny, bald-headed white man named Schultz who was, Will often said, just about as abrasive as they come. Schultz would often argue with Will, across the hedge that separated their property, about politics and boxing and baseball.

In the hot summer afternoon when Will worked in his yard, trimming and mowing and pulling weeds, he would watch Schultz out of the corner of his eye, Schultz in his ridiculous Bermuda shorts and Hawaiian-print shirt, settling himself down on his chaise longue in the shade of the fine old tree. Sometimes, on his way to his spot beneath the tree, Schultz would smile and nod to Will Capture, newspaper folded neatly under one arm, carrying a tall glass of iced lemonade, and Will would pretend that he didn't see the nod, and would not respond.

Later, from inside his house, Will would look out the window and see Schultz peacefully snoozing on the chaise longue, and he would say to himself, or to Mary Theresa, or to Cecelia, or to the walls, "It just isn't right, you know, that a man like Schultz, a man with his political views, should benefit from my tree." And Will would shake his head sadly. That went on for eight summers before Will finally decided that he would saw that tree down.

The day before Cecelia went back to California, she took a long walk, just to get out of the house and look around, to soak up some sunshine. She went downtown and looked in shop windows. She found herself in front of the Wapato Beauty Parlor and went in without making a conscious decision and told them she wanted a haircut.

This was what her mother always wanted. Snip, snip, the long hanks fell to the floor. She was reminded of when she was ten: Her mother brought her to get a haircut, after she had promised her that she could grow her hair long. "When I said you could grow it long," her mother said, "I thought I was really going to see something. I thought you were going to fix your hair in fancy hairdos. I didn't know your intention was to let it hang down all messy and ugly and hot-looking." That was how she explained her broken promise. Cecelia felt she was being led to the guillotine, and there was nothing she could do about it. Her mother controlled her completely; there was no compromise, no chance of her changing her mind, no chance of escape. Her mother said she was sick of seeing her running around looking like some wild Indian.

They cut her hair very very short. They called it an Italian cut, and she absolutely hated it. "There now, don't you feel better, all neat and cool?" She was crying. She felt as if she had been violated.

But at the age of twenty-one, she stoically watched as they snipped away.

"What I'm doing," the haircutter said, "is called layering, cutting your hair in different lengths to give it more body. Your hair is too heavy to wear long and unlayered. It gives your face too severe a look. Now, with the layering, your hair will fluff out some around your face, give you a softer look." She wanted to say to the haircutter that she didn't care about a "softer look." She wanted to say, "My hair was beautiful. It was lovely, deep dark brown, and it shone in the sun. It was beautiful hair, my best feature, and I will miss it."

As she was paying for her cut, she saw the haircutter sweep up her poor shorn hair into a dustpan and throw it into a trash can. The haircutter swept up two dustpanfuls, and still the dark dead hair lay in piles on the white tiled beauty-parlor floor.

Her mother was very pleased when she saw Cecelia with short hair. "At last," she said, smiling, "you've decided to look your age, have you?" Sometimes she despised her mother, sitting there in her wheelchair looking smug and triumphant, imagining that her ridicule had driven Cecelia to cut her beautiful hair, imagining that she still had some control over her daughter.

She didn't even bother explaining to her mother about tribal tradition—that a dead man's wife and unmarried daughters were supposed to cut their hair to show that they were in mourning. As it happened, Cecelia did not grow her hair long again. From that time on, she wore her hair in fairly short styles, sometimes even permanented. But it had nothing to do with what her mother wanted or liked.

TWELVE

Cecelia left her mother at the end of the second week, although her mother wailed that now she would be taken to the old people's home. Cecelia knew that once she was not around anymore her sisters would come and take care of Mary Theresa. She went back to California and moved into a neat, square, characterless, white-walled little apartment in student family housing. The Donahues brought Corey back to her, along with the new red tricycle they had bought for him while she was in Wapato. She enrolled him in the university day-care center and registered herself as a full-time student at Cal Berkeley.

Andrea took care of Mary Theresa after Cecelia left; then Marie arranged to take a four-month leave of absence from her job and relocated herself and her younger children in Wapato so that she could take her turn minding Mary Theresa.

Cecelia then, though she knew how much hostility and resentment she generated by not staying in Wapato, was free to go on with her life unencumbered, to move forward according to her plans.

But back in California she found that she was not the same. The sense of unreality remained with her, and she could not shake it. She went through the motions of life, attending classes and taking care of Corey, keeping everything together. One day she would feel like her old self again, she thought, and be ready to take over. Until then she had to keep her life together. Sometimes she felt like a ghost, detached and hardly there. At other times she felt afraid.

She lay alone in the dark night, unable to sleep, thinking of all the things that could go wrong. She could get sick; Corey could get sick. The San Francisco Welfare Department could track her down and carry out the threat of putting her in jail and Corey in a children's shelter. Maybe, like her father, she wouldn't be able to cut the academic mustard at the university.

She thought of how alone she was, how alone she had been all along, even before her father's death, but somehow she hadn't thought much about it. It was like the cartoon character who runs past the edge of the cliff into air, keeps on running until he suddenly realizes that he is running on air, then falls to the ground. She had no one except Corey, and he was a helpless little kid who needed her to be strong and competent, to provide him with love and a sense of security. She had to give to Corey and keep on giving, although she herself desperately needed to be given to, to be reassured, to have someone she could lean on. But there was no one for her.

She went on, faking it, meeting the demands of her studies and raising her son, although her heart was not in it. She feared she would fail soon and the whole thing, her whole too-elaborate life, would collapse and come falling down.

It was during this period that she ran into Nathan on the Berkeley campus on a bright, sunshiny early afternoon in April. She heard a man's voice call her name, and she stopped and turned. Then she saw him. He was wearing the same tan corduroy sportscoat he used to wear at CCSF, carried the same worn, leather briefcase. She remembered how the sun shone on his blond hair and how she had thought that she had never liked blond hair before, had never understood why some people found it attractive. His hair looked bright that day, and she liked it, liked the way it shone in the sun and liked his smile. Seeing him cheered her. She remembered how nice he had been to her at CCSF, the time he had spent going over the material with her. He had given her the kind of attention she needed, and she knew that she was attractive to him, not simply a student in need of academic help. She was glad to see him, glad when he asked her to lunch.

When they became lovers, she tried to hold herself aloof from him because she didn't think a man like Nathan would take her seriously. She tried to be practical. He was sexually attracted to her. She was in need of human comfort just then, wanting so much to be close to someone. She would not love him, she told herself in the beginning. She would accept what he had to offer until she felt stronger, and then she would let him go. He told her that he had been married once already. That marriage, to a surgeon's daughter, had lasted only six months, and it had soured him on the whole idea. She didn't believe him. She thought he was only telling her this so that she wouldn't expect him to marry her.

She held herself back, but only a little. She allowed herself to love him while keeping in mind that he was just temporary. Years later, remembering how she had regarded it as only a temporary liaison to help her make it through a rough time in her life, she wondered if that hadn't been what had enabled her to love him. She had overlooked things that might have bothered her otherwise. When she became irritated with him, she would remind herself that he would be out of her life soon enough, and she was thus able to love him more fully in the present.

After six months, Nathan told Cecelia that he thought it was time they parted. He didn't say why, only that it was time. She agreed. Yes, she supposed, it was time to get on down the road. She would always remember him warmly, she told him. She let him go gracefully, as she had intended that she would from the beginning, though it hurt to do so. She cried only a little, just enough to show herself and him that she truly cared. She missed him but felt relieved, too, that it was over.

She went on with her life and found that she was much stronger than she had been before Nathan came into it. She was capable now, no longer depressed and needy. Still, she didn't like the way he had been able to walk out on her. She saw the married couples all around her and remembered that she had never been married and wished that Nathan had thought her good enough to marry. She knew she would get over him, however, and she was still young. Surely she would find someone else. In the meantime she was strong enough to go on alone, to raise her son by herself. She missed Nathan nevertheless.

Two weeks after he broke off with her, when she was really beginning to feel strong again, Nathan showed up at her doorstep. He looked as if he hadn't slept in quite a long time. He was miserable without her, he said.

"Take me back, Celia," he said. "I'm no good without you." She was happy to see him, and although later she would sometimes look back on that night and wish she could somehow reverse her decision, go back to that night and tell Nathan "No, thank you," that was not how she felt at the time. She had missed him. Corey had missed him. She really did not want to be without him. She didn't want to get over him. She didn't want another man to take his place. She wanted him. They were married about a month later, and they were happy for a while, or happy enough, anyway.

THIRTEEN

The wheels of justice did not turn on Saturday and Sunday. There was nothing Cecelia could do but wait. Somehow knowing that made the waiting easier to bear. She wondered what Nathan would do now that she had called him a fucking Boy Scout and slammed the phone down in his ear. He really had been a Boy Scout, and she had called him a fucking Boy Scout before.

On Saturday morning they took her out of her cell to a shower. The shower was not nice and hot, just lukewarm, but it was better than no shower at all. They didn't give her any clothes to change into, so she had to put her blue knit dress back on. The police-woman made a helpful comment. "You might want to wash your underpants out by hand and hang them up in your cell to dry."

"Good idea," Cecelia said. "I'll do that." And she did, just as soon as she was back in her cell. Now, she thought, if I only had a magazine, I would be comfortable.

She noticed that her wrists were blue from the handcuffs. She didn't remember struggling, but she must have struggled a little, tried to break out of the handcuffs, strained against the metal. Ugly big almost-black bruises. She remembered that one other time she had bruises on her wrists, although they weren't this bad.

Nathan had given them to her, restraining her during one of their battles when she wanted to hit him. She tried to recall what that particular battle had been about.

It was the year after she graduated from college. She didn't go to law school, as she had wanted to do, because Nathan told her he didn't think she should, at least not right away. He didn't think she had the kind of mind it took to succeed at studying law. She was not swift and analytical enough, he said. Besides, it was too demanding, and she had a baby to raise now, besides a little boy. He thought it would be a good thing if she stayed home for a while. He told her he thought she should consider a more realistic career goal, such as becoming a social worker or a teacher of young children. He thought she would be more suited to a job like that than to the practice of law. Somehow he couldn't see her as a lawyer. He went on with his Ph.D. work and taught some classes, drawing money from a family scholarship. Cecelia, unable to stand being cooped up all day, day after day, enrolled in a pot-making class at an adult evening school in Berkeley. She had wanted to take macramé, but that class was full. She was bored making pots. She wanted to go to law school.

On the surface her marriage seemed to be going smoothly enough, but she had been feeling more and more not herself that year. She was drinking more, too, to relax, to keep from thinking too much, to put up with Nathan.

Nathan's background began to bother her. That was one of the things, in the beginning, that had attracted her to him. When they were first lovers she liked it that he came from a family that was socially prominent, that had everything society deemed important: money, status, political power. She was impressed that all the men in Nathan's family, from the time of the Revolutionary War, had gone to Yale. All of them except Nathan, who was different, he said, in many ways from the rest of his family. (And she supposed this was true. Not only did he not go to Yale, but he had been involved in radical politics when he was a young man. He had gotten divorced from his first wife, who was white and middle-class. And he had married a working-class Indian girl.) His family tree went all the way back to the *Mayflower,* and he had fallen heir to a sword that had belonged to one of his ancestors, who had been an officer in the Revolution (Nathan had declined to take possession of it).

She used to like to hear him tell her about his childhood. His family were Unitarians, and his parents read the children the poetry of Emerson. They were liberals, and his mother was involved in liberal political causes. His mother's oldest brother had been a senator.

When Nathan told Cecelia about his family's outings and vacations, she would imagine them and wish she had had a childhood like his. Most of all she liked his telling her about how his father, who was a concert pianist, would practice his piano into the night, and his warm memories of lying in bed and falling asleep listening to his father play. One particular piece, by Mozart, evoked this memory especially.

Now she didn't like any of those things about Nathan anymore. Not only did she no longer like them, she was bothered by them.

When she was drinking she almost hated him for his background and his happy childhood, hated the fact that as a boy he had fallen asleep listening to his father play Mozart, while she, as a child, had fallen asleep watching her mother wait for her drunken father's return and later had been awakened by the sound of her father as he came staggering home.

Most of all, she realized how condescending his attitude toward her was. He told her, in the early days of their affair, that he had never experienced such passion before, except when he was a very young man and had spent a year traveling in Mexico and South America. In Guadalajara he had gone to a whorehouse, and he had imagined himself in love with a beautiful prostitute there. Her name was Lupe. He became obsessed with Lupe. Once he got drunk and went to the whorehouse, bringing one dozen red roses, and proposed to Lupe. She knew that he was drunk, of course, and didn't mean it. She teased him that he would first have to convert to Catholicism (Lupe always wore a little silver crucifix on a chain around her neck) and Nathan had said he would never do a thing like that. He couldn't even be a Unitarian anymore—he was an atheist. But he never forgot Lupe, and he never expected he would find such passion again, but he had.

Now Cecelia began to realize that he looked down on her. He didn't think she had the right kind of mind to study law. She reminded him of Lupe. When she first told him that she had begun college without graduating from high school, he said, "And you didn't have to take remedial English?" He looked down on her and thought she was less intelligent than he, and maybe that was why he felt such passion for her in the beginning, maybe that was part of why he married her. Whatever it was, she was not happy with him anymore, and she often seethed with resentment toward him.

One night they went to San Francisco to an all-white party, and Cecelia began drinking because she was bored. She had taken a bottle of wine and sat looking out the window in the front room, her back to the party. The apartment where the party was held was high in the hills near the San Francisco Medical Center, on the third story of a fine old house. She felt high in the sky in her window seat.

She looked at the stately old restored nineteenth-century houses across the street and the lights spreading below. She watched the fog roll in. Now and then she looked at the surface of the window, at the reflection of the partygoers behind her. White people. She didn't belong there, she thought. It was as if she did not belong to her own life anymore. She had so painstakingly constructed this life for herself, and now she didn't belong to it. Her soul did not belong to it.

She overheard an exchange between Nathan and Tracy. Tracy was her friend, so-called, the one who was giving the party. They were making a pun on the Dee Brown book *Bury My Heart at Wounded Knee*, which was on the *New York Times* bestseller list then. She had given a copy to Nathan, but he wouldn't read it.

Nathan had some kind of minor knee injury, and he and Tracy were making a joke. "Oh, wounded knee, as in bury my heart at," she heard Tracy say, and she and Nathan laughed. They were all laughing, these merry partygoers, at different little jokes. That is what parties were for, she supposed, for people to get together with other people and laugh about stupid jokes, to entertain one another.

But that one, that joke, "wounded knee, as in bury my heart at," and the laughter that followed it, she didn't like. The laughter was shrill and irritating. But they didn't know. She took another drink. She lit a cigarette, watched herself take a drag from it, move it down, rest it on her knee. Like her mother watching out the window in Idaho. Her mother's gesture. They didn't know about Wounded Knee. Surely they didn't.

Wounded Knee was not so long ago. There were photographs of the massacre. It happened long after the battles, long after the treaties were signed. Cecelia had seen those old photographs. They were much worse than anything she had seen from My Lai. The Indian bodies lay frozen in the snow, and they were not the bodies of warriors. They were all kinds of people: old people, women, children. None of them was armed. They were gunned down by the U.S. Army at Wounded Knee.

She remembered the photographs of the communal grave, the long trench the soldiers dug and piled the bodies into. She had read accounts of how the white soldiers had not only taken articles of clothing and jewelry and scalps but had cut genitals and other body parts off the corpses as well, souvenirs to bring home from Wounded Knee. She drank more. She got drunker and drunker, and she continued to watch the party in the reflection in the window glass. She hated that no-good Tracy. She hated them all. Most of all, she hated her own husband.

Cecelia drank so much that the battle she and Nathan had when they got home that night was never really clear in her memory; she remembered only snatches here and there.

She had called him "a fucking Boy Scout" and said, "Those Indian kids who gave you the finger sure had the right idea." She was alluding to an incident in his boyhood he had told her about. To get to Many Pines Boy Scout Camp, the bus had to travel across an Indian reservation. Once a group of Indian boys had been waiting for the bus, and when they saw it coming, they lined up single file along the road, and as the bus passed, they all raised their hands, giving the middle-finger salute.

"You thought you could play Mister Big with your stupid little squaw, didn't you? Well, you've got another think coming, Buster."

And he had barked back that he had given her everything: a house in the suburbs, two cars, a washer and drier. Look where she was now and where she had been when he met her. She didn't have a thing he hadn't given her. And now she had this nice little family and she was trying to fuck it all up, a nice little family that went on trips to Canada and Disneyland and Mexico and spent weekends in Tahoe, and she bought all those stupid clothes she didn't even need at I. Magnin and had her hair done at some San Francisco salon. She'd never even had a real job. In all of her life she'd never had a thing that wasn't given to her.

She wanted to kill him. She pounded him with her fists and called him a big failure of a Boy Scout, and he grabbed her by the wrists and twisted them. She didn't feel any pain at the time. She looked into his face and saw the face of Jimmy Griffith, the white boy back in Lodi, Idaho, who had thrown her down the stairs at school. The baby woke up and began to cry. Cecelia imagined Nicole with her face all scrunched up and tears flowing from her eyes as she stood hanging on to the side of her crib in the dark room. She was probably very frightened.

Corey stood quietly in the doorway watching Nathan and Cecelia hurting each other. Damned white man, she said. He said she was nothing but a drunk, all she ever was, all she'd ever be. Just like her dad. She had stopped fighting him then, and he let go of her and went to tend to the children. She lay on the floor, drunk and miserable, and cried.

When he came back to her, when the children were settled in their beds, he helped her to her feet and took her to the big chair and held her in his lap, and she cried and cried. He had whispered to her that he loved her. Please don't cry, he had said, shhhhhh, it's all right now. Don't cry.

The next morning he took them on a family outing, insisted on it, even though she had a terrible hangover. They went to the Berkeley Marina and walked on the pier. He was trying to be cheerful, and the children seemed not to be suffering too much psychological harm from the horrible scene they had witnessed the night before. They went to Port Coata and had dinner in a funky renovated warehouse and toured Muriel's Dollhouse. They bought ice-cream cones at Baskin-Robbins.

By the end of the day everything had apparently returned to normal. Cecelia was enjoying herself in spite of her hangover. She joked with Corey, cuddled Nicole on her lap. Nathan said, "That's the first time I've seen you smile all day. Do you know how good that makes me feel? Do you know how important to me it is that you're happy? I love you, Cecelia."

After the children were in bed that night, he told her he wanted her never to drink again. She told him that she would not promise that. He had no right. He was always trying to control her, she said, and she didn't like it.

"All right, then, Cecelia. You may not know it, but after a few drinks you undergo a drastic personality change. You just aren't yourself anymore. It's as if you become someone else, and I feel helpless. All I can do then is wait for you to come back, for my real wife to return to me. Do this for me, will you? Don't drink around me. Ever. I don't know if I can take much more of it. I mean it. I'm serious."

She knew what he meant. He meant that he would probably leave her. She wasn't angry at him anymore. The fight seemed stupid now. She didn't like the thought of having to raise two children all by herself. She would probably be very poor again, too. She didn't want him to leave her.

She thought of what he had said, that she became a different person. That was what she used to think about her mother when she had one of her crazy spells, when she hated Cecelia and Cecelia's father and the whole reservation and imagined they were all against her.

It had been awful. And all she had been able to do was wait for her real mother to come back, to return to herself.

She nodded to her husband. "All right, Nathan, I promise. I won't drink around you anymore." There was one other matter, and although she didn't know if this was the right time to be bringing it up, she did.

"I want something, too, Nathan."

"What?"

"I want to go to law school."

"No, you don't. You just think you do." She felt a dark cloud pass over her heart, and the anger, the resentment toward him rose in her blood again. He obviously could see the anger. Now he was the one who nodded.

"All right, Cecelia. Go ahead. You know you will have to take the LSAT examination, and it's very rough. You might not even be accepted by a good law school."

"Yes, I will, Nathan," she said.

He didn't answer.

She had kept her promise not to drink around him. She didn't drink at all for a while, but as the marriage became more of a burden and the pressures increased, she began to drink away from him and come home under the influence. Her marriage had been going bad for a very long time.

FOURTEEN

Sunday she was allowed to have another shower, and she washed her underpants again and hung them over one of the faucets to dry.

Monday morning, after breakfast, a policewoman came and got her and took her out of her cell.

"Where are you taking me? Not court, I hope. I want to look better than this when I go to court."

"I'm taking you to check you out. Someone's paid your bail."

Nathan. It could be no one else.

She saw him waiting in the little area beside the glassed-in checkout room. He wasn't watching for her. He was reading a newspaper. She was surprised at how old and tired he looked. He didn't look thirty-seven. He looked as if he were in his forties. He didn't look like a man who would be her husband. He looked more like her dad. Maybe that was what she had really wanted him to be, her adopted dad. She was the kid; he was the dad. Maybe that was one reason why letting go of the marriage was so difficult. She was a thirty-year-old delinquent.

In the checkout room, a fat, doughy-faced cop gave her back her watch and the contents of her handbag, which they had put into a manila envelope. She had to examine each item in the envelope and check off a list and sign for the return of her belongings.

"Officer," she said when she was all ready to go, "may I see my mugshots?"

"Sure, lady," the cop said. He opened the folder to the three glossy black-and-white photographs of her face and handed the folder to her.

Cecelia examined the pictures. One was from the front, one was from the right, and one was from the left. It was the photo from the front that interested her. She didn't look obviously drunk or disheveled, but what struck her was the expression on her face.

She was reminded of one night when she was a little girl in Idaho. She had gone with her father to investigate a commotion in the chicken house. Her father brought his .22. They cornered the weasel before he could reach the tunnel he had dug under the fence. Her father gave her the flashlight to hold, making her, then, his accomplice. She had often been her father's accomplice.

Her face in the mugshots looked like that weasel's face.

"Damned chicken-murdering weasel," her father had muttered, taking careful aim.

The weasel stared straight into the bright light, and his eyes gleamed. He had been cornered in the chicken yard in the night, caught almost in the act. Now he gazed calmly, steadily into the light Cecelia held on him, perfectly still, poised as if to run.

In the case of the chicken-murdering weasel there had been no plea bargaining. Nobody cared about extenuating circumstances. That weasel had no constitutional rights and was as guilty as sin. The weasel had had his head blown away, and Cecelia had had to watch because it was her job to hold the light steady while her father performed the execution.

She closed the file containing the mugshots and handed it back to the policeman and thanked him. Then she left the checkout room and went to face her husband.

Cecelia and Nathan didn't speak to each other at all at first. Neither made any move to touch the other. He looked unbearably weary to her. She felt unbearably grubby. Finally it was she who spoke first.

"I don't want to talk just now, Nathan. They've had me here since Thursday night."

"Yes, I know," he said.

"Do you want to talk today, or can it wait until morning?"

"No, not tomorrow. Today."

"Then let me go home and bathe and change my clothes. Give me a couple of hours to readjust to being outside a jail cell."

He nodded. He looked away, avoiding her eyes, toward the checkout room.

"Where do you want to meet?" he asked.

"How about the International House of Pancakes, on University Avenue? My apartment building is just across the street from there. . . . Unless you would rather come to my apartment . . ."

He shook his head. "The pancake house will be fine," he said. "Do you know where your car is?"

"Yes. It isn't a long walk from here. I'll drive myself home. Shall we say in three hours, then?"

"That'll be fine."

They walked out of the courthouse together, without looking at each other or speaking, and down the steps to the sidewalk.

It was raining outside, and this seemed to help some. Cecelia thought she would have felt seedier if the sun had been shining and a lot of people had been out enjoying the day. It was afternoon, however. She would have felt better yet if it had been night and she could have slunk through the shadows on the way to her car.

The car started right up. The traffic was not too heavy on the way back to the apartment. It took less than half an hour to drive across town.

Her apartment was an ungodly mess, of course, just as she had left it. She took *Black's Law Dictionary* out of the window it had been propping open. The book was ruined, partly soaked to pulp. She held it for a minute, remembering her first year of law school and how she had to consult that dictionary every day because she didn't know legal terms and had never taken Latin, She hardly needed it anymore.

She had two and a half hours to prepare to meet Nathan. She got busy and put the apartment in order, picked up all the news magazines and *Gilbert's* outlines and either piled them up and put them away or took them to the garbage chute at the end of the hall. In the course of her cleaning she ran across a slip of paper with an old phone number she had forgotten she had. It said: Thomas Running Horse, Roseberg, Oregon. She remembered Running Horse and smiled. She wished she could have had more of Running Horse.

FIFTEEN

They moved to Spokane so that Nathan could accept a teaching job there. They moved into a two-story house with a large yard not far from a shopping center. Nathan said he was glad to be gone from the Bay Area with its overcrowding, filthy air, and high crime rate. But Cecelia hated Spokane. To Nathan it was clean and wholesome. Life was easier there. No more bumper-to-bumper traffic to put up with, no scarcity of parking places. Spokane had space and fresh air, was a good place to raise a family. To Cecelia it was slow, stupid, and dull. Being there reminded her of her childhood. All their neighbors were white and she felt that she and Nathan were noticed and not approved of as a racially mixed couple, an oddity in those parts. Nathan said that was nonsense. Just her imagination. She tried to adjust to Spokane, tried to see positive things about it. But the memory of California was too strong. She thought of it daily, as homesick immigrants will recall the old country. She longed for the fresh, polluted air of the Bay Area.

When Nathan first told her about the job in Spokane, she considered not going with him. Maybe this is how it will end, she thought, and the notion frightened her. She was afraid of being poor again. And she thought her reasons for wanting to separate from Nathan were in fact rather frivolous. He worked, and he didn't drink. He didn't run around with other women or use dope.

He didn't beat her. She should try harder, she thought, to over-look his shortcomings—his coldness, for instance, his mean-spirit-edness and his condescending attitude. And what if she *was* lonely. Maybe that was the way people were supposed to be. Nobody had a perfect marriage, after all, and theirs was certainly not as bad as some.

She thought she should transfer to Gonzaga School of Law and said she would do that, although it didn't have nearly the reputa-tion of Boalt Hall. She could still complete her degree there. But she kept putting off applying. Then it was too late, and she stayed at home all winter, withdrew into herself, felt a terrible sadness. She began to feel the way she imagined her mother must have felt when Cecelia was a little girl, caught fast in a trap of her own making (and that it was of her own making made it all the harder to break out of), doomed to live with a man she didn't feel connected to anymore, to live her life almost as if the same day kept repeating itself over and over. She was the prisoner now, as Mary Theresa had been, of circumstance and an inability to imagine anything beyond the prison, to create anything different for herself.

She and Nathan hardly spoke to each other now. The children didn't appear to be affected by the coldness between their par-ents. When she remembered that awful time she would think that they must have been affected by it. They probably just chose to ignore it. She and Nathan slept together still, and they con-tinued to have sex every third or fourth night, according to the pattern they had established years before. It was a habit they didn't try to break, even though they no longer lay in each other's arms, snuggling and talking, maintaining their bond.

Nathan would initiate it late at night when she was almost asleep by reaching over and fondling one of her breasts. His touch would be tentative, as if he expected her to reject his advances. When she didn't he would lift her nightgown or pajama top and, leaning over her, take first one nipple in his mouth and then the other. She would respond then, as she always did. Her nipples would stand up plump and erect as they always had, in spite of her feelings toward him now. He wouldn't kiss her mouth or hold her close. She would not put her arms around him as he mounted her. There was no tenderness between them. It would be over quickly, and she would always have an orgasm, as would he, but she never felt satisfied. The sex act was always performed in silence in the dead of night, and the attitude of each was as if they were thieves or copractitioners of some secret, awful rite that they had agreed not to mention. This isn't real, she would think sometimes after their sex as they lay in their queen-sized bed in the darkened bedroom, backs turned to each other. This isn't the way a marriage is supposed to be. It was then she would feel most lonely of all, when she would wish most profoundly that she had a soul mate, a man who would love and cherish and take care of her. But after a while this stopped, too, and all feelings, including loneliness, receded.

Most of the time it was all right this way and she didn't think much about anything. She didn't feel bad. She was an adequate mother, she would think when she cooked her children's dinner, or in the mornings when Nicole stood on a chair while she braided her hair, or when she went to pick up Nicole at the Bluebirds' meeting. Corey was growing up, though, and with Corey it was harder to be adequate. He played loud rock music and flunked math. His manner became sullen. He ran around with a gang of seedy-looking teenage boys. She wasn't sure that everything was all right with him. She would feel anxious about Corey. He was so sweet when he was little and so cute. He wasn't supposed to turn into a hood now. She didn't know how to reach him. Maybe he didn't need reaching. Maybe he was really all right. Sometimes an awareness would descend on her that here she was twenty-nine years old and she didn't have much of a life, didn't have much of a future to look forward to, other than her children growing up and leaving her and she and Nathan growing old.

"Did you ever apply to Gonzaga?" Nathan asked her one morning as they sat with toast and coffee at the kitchen table. She shook her head without looking at him. She had just finished reading her horoscope, which said to get ready for romance. She was now reading "Dear Abby." The column that day was all about how wives should forgive their husbands' adultery. "You should, you know," Nathan said. "You really should do something." His tone said that she was useless. She was boring. She didn't much care what he thought.

Later that same day she felt a nagging ache in the joint of her right shoulder, and when she went to lift the garbage can to carry it out to the alley she found that the pain prevented her. She realized immediately what it was, and a cold feeling spread over her. Arthritis. She had Mary Theresa's crippling ailment. She had to do something now. She had to do it quickly and break out of this oppressive situation. She called the law school in Berkeley that afternoon and found she could be reinstated by August and would be eligible for a scholarship if she was separated from her husband, which she said she was. She would have to apply for it right away, though. She said she would mail the form back the same day it arrived. She took two aspirins. By evening the pain in her shoulder had disappeared.

Nathan didn't get home until very late that night. He had made friends with people he met through the college, and he was often late coming home. She told him in the morning that she was going to go to Berkeley, and he said nothing. Just nodded.

"Can you manage without me?" she asked.

"Of course. Go ahead. Go back to Berkeley and finish your degree. We'll be fine." She thought he seemed relieved. She went ahead and made plans, was reinstated, was granted the scholarship for the fall. Life became better.

She bought marigolds and primroses and pansies and other simple, sturdy flowers that could be stuck in the ground and watered. Her appetite returned, and she gained five, ten, finally fifteen pounds.

Nathan no longer reached to touch her breasts in the dead of night, and she was surprised to find she missed those loveless sexual encounters. She reached over and touched him one night, and his breathing seemed to stop. He lay perfectly still as she caressed his bare shoulder, his chest, his stomach. Then he caught her hand and pushed it away, shifted in the bed, turned his back to her. She felt deeply humiliated and angry. Neither of them said a word then or mentioned it later. They were never to have sex with each other again.

The morning she left Spokane, the children went off to school as usual. Nicole had tears in her eyes as she hugged and kissed her mother good-bye. "I'll be back soon, Nicole."

"I know, Mom. But I can't help it. I feel sad."

She held Nicole close. She would be with her again soon. It wasn't as if it was forever. Corey was nonchalant. She had to ask him to kiss her, and then he just gave her a quick little peck on the cheek. He was as tall as she was now and growing fast. Cecelia asked Nathan if he would meet her downtown at noon and have lunch with her, since she would be gone for nine months.

Cecelia spent the morning packing the Ford with her belongings. She had even bought herself a twenty-dollar black-and-white television set at an auction. By noon the car was loaded with clothes, books, typewriter and other essentials.

She was five minutes late meeting Nathan. He wasn't there. She wasn't sure that he had even come until later, when she called him and he told her he had thought she had probably decided to get started right away instead of having lunch. So it was with bad feelings that she left Spokane.

The Ford died in a small town in northern Oregon. It caught fire somewhere underneath, and she pulled into a rest stop and put out the fire with water from a hose. She was thinking about saving her belongings. Later a man told her that that was the worst thing she could have done; she should have gotten away, because the whole thing could easily have exploded when she doused it with water. She had lost hours and then had to find another car she could afford. She finally settled on a drab green second-hand Chevy. The money that she spent was supposed to have supported her until she got her first scholarship check. She worried about how she was going to make ends meet now. But she knew she would manage somehow. She always did, didn't she?

She ended up having to spend the night in a motel in northern Oregon and slept a long, exhausted sleep and ate a leisurely breakfast and felt grateful that she was free and didn't have to answer to anyone but herself. She felt almost giddy with freedom. No more wondering why Nathan wouldn't speak to her or why he didn't want to have sex with her or what was wrong with her that her own husband would be so unresponsive to her. It was almost as if Nathan really didn't exist any more. She took her time driving south. She stopped at a few historical markers and rested and looked around, went to a pioneer museum. She bought herself a cup of coffee and a local paper in one small town and took an hour drinking coffee, having a refill, then another, and reading her paper. She could do just about anything, she thought, that she felt like doing.

That afternoon she was heading toward Roseberg. One sign said, "Roseberg via the freeway." Another sign said, "Roseberg via the lake." Cecelia decided to take the more scenic route, via the lake, thinking that it would be pleasant and there was no reason why she shouldn't.

It was certainly more scenic, but it was a hundred miles farther up into the mountains and the woods. There were no filling stations and hardly any other cars on the road. When the gas gauge registered empty, Cecelia left the main road and turned up a little dirt road that looked as if it had been traveled recently. At the end of the road she found a ranger's station and two rangers. They siphoned gas from one of their vehicles and poured it into the Chevy, refusing the money she tried to give them. It was the first time in a very long while, she realized, that she had been alone and in danger and had had to take care of herself, although she had once been very used to doing so. She was really on her own now, and this was just the beginning.

It was late when she finally got into Roseberg, and she was tired and hungry. She found a bar next to the filling station, a down-home country and western type of place with a dance band and sawdust on the floor. She went inside and proceeded to drink. They didn't have good wine at this bar, just Spañada and Annie Greensprings, so she drank pink squirrels and margaritas and piña coladas and other cocktails that satisfied her hunger as they pushed away the panic.

As she drank, she began to feel better. It didn't matter anymore about Nathan's not being a good husband. It didn't matter that her car had broken down and she'd had to spend her rent money buying an old clunker. It didn't matter that she was on her way to go live alone in Berkeley for nine months.

The tavern filled up, and the band played country music, and it was not a bad place to be. A man asked her to dance with him, and she did, and it was fun. She hadn't danced in years, she realized. Not long after that, another man asked her to dance. She was having a good time, and she began to wish that she had tried to look more attractive, that she'd dressed up and worn makeup.

Then she saw *him* standing at the bar. He was an Indian. Unmistakably. A handsome, dark-eyed, brown-skinned Indian with hair as black as night. He was very tall, more than six feet two, and his build was strong and athletic. He was dressed cowboy-style, like many of the men in the tavern. When he turned his back, she could see that he wore a belt with his name tooled into it. She couldn't read the name from across the room. She thought that the fancy silver belt buckle was a champion rodeo rider's, but she couldn't be sure.

She wished she still looked the way she did when she was eighteen. But he noticed her anyway, of course. He would have had to notice her, since she and he were the only two skins in the place.

He was talking to another man and a blond woman with a frizzy hairdo who was all dressed up like a cowgirl, but he kept looking at Cecelia, and she kept looking back. The waitress brought her a margarita, "from the tall man at the bar in the black Stetson hat."

He looked more and more attractive to her. His face was classic. He would have to be a Sioux, she thought, with those strong, chiseled features. He was a Sioux, as it turned out, from the Rocky Boy Reservation. The name tooled on the back of his belt was Thomas, but she would call him only by his last name, Running Horse.

Running Horse came and asked her to dance when the band played a slow song. It was a hit by the King of Country Music, George Jones, "He Stopped Loving Her Today."

He said, "I'll love you till I die."
She told him, "You'll forget in time."

It felt good to be in his arms. Very tall men sometimes perceived her as being very tall, much taller than she actually was.

Indian men weren't supposed to have beards, the way other men do. That was what those Old West movies would have you believe. She knew that this was often true, and she decided to test Running Horse. She leaned up close to touch her face against his, and in so doing pressed her breasts against his chest, and she knew that he could feel her breath on his neck. She liked the smell of his cologne or aftershave or whatever it was, just barely there. She was delighted when she felt his arms tighten around her and his breathing become a bit heavier. His face *was* very smooth. She knew that his chest would be like that, too, smooth, hairless, or almost hairless.

He was graceful, very graceful for a big man wearing clunky cowboy boots. His lead was strong and sure, not just simple back-and-forth steps either, but fancy stuff, turns and dips.

He stopped loving her today.
They placed a wreath upon his door,
And soon they'll carry him away.
He stopped loving her today.

She couldn't remember the last time she had felt so powerfully attracted to a man. But she recognized that feeling. Then she remembered Bud. That was long ago, but it was the last time she had felt so free and mellow. She felt more alive in Running Horse's embrace than she had for a long time.

She knew that later on Running Horse would ask her to go home with him, and when he did she would say yes. Before that he told her something about himself. He had left Montana at the age of seventeen to join the paratroops, and he had no family. His silver buckle was won bull riding. He was forty years old. She hadn't even thought about his age. Forty sounded so old, yet he was not "too old" for her. He worked at the lumber mill in Roseberg.

Running Horse had beautiful hands, she thought, big, strong, heavily veined hands. Her father had had hands like that. Her father told her, when she was a little girl, that his veins were like that because he was a full-blood. Cecelia was pushing thirty now, and she had never slept with an Indian man. Only white men.

She told Running Horse the truth about herself, that she was a married woman en route to Berkeley to finish her law degree. He had trouble with the last part of that.

"Do you mean to become a legal secretary or something?"

"To become a lawyer."

"A lawyer? A mouthpiece? You mean you're going to be one of those guys who goes to court and tells the judge what's going on and then writes motions and briefs and things?"

"Yeah."

"Well, I'll be damned!"

On the way to his apartment Running Horse reached a hand over and touched her as he drove, stroked her arm, her hand.

"Your skin is so soft," he said, "so smooth, so soft." She felt mildly, pleasantly aroused. She wanted to be with him. She was glad she was. She wished that Nathan could see her.

"You gonna be a lawyer, huh?"

"Yeah."

"Well, that's okay. You're a pretty woman. Damned pretty woman you are, just the same. I did sort of think, before you told me you were gonna be a lawyer, that you talked awful funny."

"That I talked funny? What do you mean?"

"Like you study that 'Increase Your Word Power' in *Reader's Digest.* I always did think there's nothing much worse than an educated squaw." He was smiling a teasing kind of smile at her. "Now, don't go getting mad, honey, 'cause I like you fine." But she didn't like it.

Once they got into bed together, she felt no desire for him at all. She was afraid. He took her in his arms and kissed her, and she could feel his erection press against her. She pulled away from him.

"Look, I'm sorry, but I can't," she said, fully realizing the vulnerability of her position, lying naked in bed with a man in Oregon. It was ridiculous. She knew that she would probably have to whether she wanted to or not. It wouldn't be hard for him, either, a big, strong man like him, and Cecelia as drunk as she was.

He didn't try to force himself on her, though. He gently stroked her hair, gently kissed her forehead, her face.

"What is it, honey?" Running Horse asked, whispering. "What's wrong with my honey?" Honey, he called her. She liked being called honey by him even though she knew that it was probably because he couldn't remember her name.

She lay resting her head on his chest, which was as smooth as she had known that it would be. She touched his face, liking so much the fact that he had hardly any beard. She was reminded of when she was very young, four or five years old. She would sometimes become frightened in the night, because of a bad dream or sometimes because of a thunderstorm. She would go get into bed with her father. Her parents had separate rooms. She had only very vague memories of their ever having slept together.

Her father's face was smooth like Running Horse's, and she would touch her cheek against his. She would ask him to tell her Coyote stories. Coyote stories, according to tribal belief, had strong power. The telling of Coyote stories could change the weather—that was why it was important to begin telling them only when the weather was at its very worst, because the weather could then change only for the better. Coyote stories also had the power to keep away evil. Mostly they had the power to make a frightened little girl feel secure and safe again.

Running Horse was kissing her, sweet little kisses. She ran her hand over his chest. Broad, muscular bull-rider's, lumberjack's chest. He caught her hand, kissed it, touched her wedding ring, making both of them suddenly aware of it and her married status.

"Is that it, honey? Is it your old man?" Running Horse asked. "Are you feeling bad about him?"

184

"No," she said. She would not allow herself to feel bad about Nathan, not this time she wouldn't.

"Have you done this before?" he asked her. "I mean have you ever slept with another man while you were married?"

"Yes," she lied. "I certainly have. Many times." She wished that that were true. She recalled all those lonely nights she had spent beside Nathan and the way he treated her and the love he no longer gave her. She should have done it with a lot of other men. She would now.

Her desire for Running Horse returned, then, when she recalled Nathan's indifference and how long she'd hungered for love, to be held by a man and wanted in the way Running Horse wanted her now. She pushed misgivings and regrets aside and lay still in his arms, savoring the ordinary, longed-for pleasures of sex: the nearness and warmth of his body, the feel of his rough, calloused hands on her smooth thighs. She returned his kisses and allowed the sexual excitement to rise and take over. No more talking. No more thinking. Only this most intense of physical pleasures. Being lifted away somewhere where she was free. A dream. There she was riding a horse across a big, grassy field, riding against the wind, the sunlight on her face, riding harder and harder still, galloping, rushing against the wind astride her running horse. When she came it was in a great explosion and seemed to last a long time. She leaned forward and rested her face against his chest. Gradually she drifted downward into ordinary consciousness. She felt good now. Satisfied. Her tensions and doubts and bad feeling were all washed away. She lay in his arms and enjoyed his stroking her hair, kissing her face. She said his name softly. "Running Horse," she said, "Running Horse."

"Are you always like that?" he asked. She didn't know what he meant. It didn't make sense to her. She didn't answer him. She was aware of being very tired now. She didn't want to talk. All she wanted was to lie cradled in his arms while she drifted off.

He fell asleep before she did, though. She could tell by his heavy, even breathing. He slept soundly while she continued for a time to drift in an aimless, warm, half-conscious state.

She thought a silly thought: Before there was anyone else on this continent, before Vikings, before the *Mayflower,* before the Spanish conquistadores, before the African slave ships, before Ellis Island and its famous huddled masses and all the others, before any of them, their ancestors were here, hers and Running Horse's, and maybe a thousand years ago their ancestors knew each other, a man and a woman who found each other beautiful, and maybe they slept together like this in each other's arms, a man and a woman together somewhere in a teepee on the Great Plains, covered with a buffalo robe, lying as they were now. Running Horse would have made a good man for her back in those days, she thought, as strong as he was. He would have been a good protector, a good hunter of buffalo.

In the dim early-morning light they made love again, and she saw that their skin tones were almost the same. No, they were exactly the same, and she felt happy because it felt right in a way it never had been before with any other man, even with Brian Donahue, because this man, this dumb, uneducated skin, this cowboy-cum-lumberjack could understand her soul in a way no white man ever could, ever, not even the husband she had once loved and had slept with almost every night for eight years.

This man knew what it was like to be a reservation kid, he knew about being outside mainstream society, and he knew about poverty and Indian pride. He told her that he had no family of his own, but she could bet that he would understand what it was like to have a father who was a sad drunkard.

Nathan didn't understand what graduating from Berkeley meant to her, since to him graduating college was simply a matter of course. But this man she had just met could understand, even if he did make an unfunny joke about "educated squaws."

Running Horse called in sick at work the next morning, and they slept until noon. Then they went down to Sambo's for a pancake-and-bacon breakfast. After they had eaten, he walked her to her car and kissed her good-bye and gave her the slip of paper with his phone number written on it and told her the next time she came through Roseberg she was welcome to spend the night with him. She hated to leave him. She wanted to stay right there in Roseberg with him, wanted to be whatever it was he might want his woman to be.

"You were supposed to be impressed," she told him after she had gotten into her car. Though it was still August, the morning was brisk, and it seemed like autumn.

"Oh, I was, honey. I was *real* impressed. Couldn't you tell?" He smiled, leaning his elbows on the edge of the car near the window. She loved his face, his Indian face. She thought she could have loved him if things had been different somehow.

"You were supposed to be impressed that I'm going to be a lawyer, turkey," she said, and he winked at her. Then he stepped away from the car so that she could drive off.

She felt sad about having left him, and she tried not to think about him. She switched the car radio away from country and western to "easy listening." She had one disturbing thought: There he was in that redneck bar. If she hadn't come along, he probably would have wound up with some funky white broad, maybe that no-class, frizzy-haired blond she saw him talking to.

Cecelia remembered Running Horse now as she found the slip of paper with his name and phone number written on it. Running Horse of Roseberg, Oregon. She had kept his phone number, even though she had no intention of calling him and knew that she never would. She put the slip of paper away in a dresser drawer. Maybe instead of throwing it away she would just leave it when she moved.

She wondered, if he had lived in Berkeley, or if she had stayed in Roseberg, if she could have found a way to stay there, would she have continued with Running Horse? Would she be his woman now? A foolish thought. A poor choice he would have been, a man who went to bars and drank and chased women. But maybe that night in Oregon was the night her marriage really ended. Maybe her sleeping with Running Horse was the ceremony that marked the end.

She had to hurry now. She didn't have much time left to bathe, wash and dry her hair, make herself up, and dress to meet Nathan.

She was a few minutes late. Nathan was already there, seated at a booth near the far windows when she arrived. He waved her over. He didn't look any more rested than he had when she'd seen him several hours earlier. He looked worse, if that was possible. His face was gaunt and pale. He didn't look at her, not directly, after she sat down.

A waitress poured her coffee and went away. She didn't ask if Cecelia wanted to see a menu. Nathan had probably already told her that they wouldn't be eating. Just coffee. That's all. She sipped her coffee and waited for him to speak.

"I want a divorce," he said, looking out the window. She joined him in looking out the window, as if there were anything to see out there besides the nearly empty parking lot.

"Of course, Nathan," she said.

"I want custody of Nicole."

"Why?"

"Because I think she'll be better off with me."

She was about to say she didn't think that was true, then stopped herself. She didn't know what was going to happen. She couldn't take custody of anyone right then.

"Maybe she would be, Nathan, but only for now. Not for good."

"Do you want joint custody? I don't think you should try to do that, Cecelia."

"I think maybe joint custody. Maybe we should let our lawyers discuss this issue and all the issues. What we can settle right now is that we both want a divorce."

He nodded, meeting her eyes for only an instant, then shifting his gaze to the other side of the room. "I'll keep Corey, too, until you finish your law degree and find a job."

"I'll have to study for the bar, then take the examination. The results aren't known for months."

"I know. I'll keep him for you until you do all that and find a job."

"Maybe that wouldn't be a good idea, Nathan, with things the way they are. Maybe Corey should go live in El Sobrante for a while."

Nathan shrugged. "Maybe so. It's really up to you. But Corey isn't doing well in school, as you know. I think maybe he should stay in Spokane and finish the school year there. It might be better than his going to live with the Donahues for a few months, then having to change schools again. I think you should think about what's best for Corey." His voice had a slightly self-righteous tone. He didn't know that Nicole had told her about Corey's mishaps in Spokane.

"I'll need some more time, Nathan, to think about that. About Corey, I mean. I'll call you next week."

"Do you want to file, or should I?" he asked.

She smiled. She didn't know why some women wanted to be the ones to file for divorce, as though it were important to them to be the ones divorcing rather than the ones being divorced.

"You file, Nathan. I think Washington divorce laws are a bit neater and less costly. Let me know who your lawyer is; then I'll select mine."

She looked at her watch as if she had an important appointment and said, "Oh, it's getting late. I've got to run. Good-bye, Nathan."

"Good-bye," he said, just glancing at her. She left him sitting in the pancake house and returned to her apartment to sleep a long and dreamless sleep.

__Sixteen

Cecelia saw the lawyer who worked for the Berkeley public defender's office the morning after she got out of jail. He was a cheerful young man with good manners.

"What is the worst that can happen?" she asked him.

"Don't worry," he said. "The worst won't happen."

"Just tell me what the maximum penalty is."

"Six months in the county jail. A five-thousand-dollar fine. But that won't happen. I don't see any way that it could. Don't worry."

"I see."

"I think you'll probably get off without having to do any jail time. It's your first offense, after all, and not too large an amount. The judge will take all that into account when he does the sentencing. If you do get any time, it'll probably be only two or three weeks. Hardly more than a slap on the wrist. Then you'll have to make arrangements to pay back the eleven hundred dollars you owe the state and be put on probation for a period of not more than one year. It isn't going to be bad. You'll see." He smiled what was intended as a reassuring smile. "Now then, do you want to plead guilty to the driving-under-the-influence charge? You'd better. They've got evidence that you were very intoxicated when they picked you up."

"Yes," she said, "I want to plead guilty to that. I was guilty."

She knew, though, that no matter what the young man said, she would probably not get off easily. That was not going to happen. She knew it. Besides, she didn't think going to jail for two or three weeks was getting off easy. She didn't want to go to jail at all. Not ever again. And then there was the matter of the bar's regarding welfare fraud as "a crime of moral turpitude." She wouldn't be allowed to practice law.

That same day Cecelia went to the gun shop in El Cerrito right across from McFarlane's Candy and Ice-Cream Store and tried to buy a gun. The proprietor asked her why she wanted one, and she gave the answer she had prepared ahead of time: "I work nights. I have to ride a bus and then walk six long dark blocks. I get scared. I need it for self-defense."

"Where do you work?"

"At the Post Office. Rincon Avenue."

He gave her forms to fill out to apply to the state for a gun permit. Then, he told her, there would be a two-week waiting period while they checked her job and personal references and made sure she did not have a criminal record. She could pick up the gun in fifeen days. Even in this she was thwarted. Would she have to throw herself in front of a truck, she wondered, or jump out her apartment window, or try something else less private than a simple gun?

She walked out of the shop in a kind of despair. "Pssst," said someone in her ear. She turned. He was shifty-eyed, unshaven, and his dirty shoulder-length hair was uncombed. He wore a shabby oversized overcoat. "Wanna buy a gun?" he whispered, glancing quickly up and down the street. "What kind you want? I got a couple I can sell you. How many you want?"

"I want a revolver," she said.

So it was easy after all.

She didn't buy any bullets. She would wait until after she went to court to buy bullets. The judge would give her time to put her affairs in order. She felt immensely comforted after she bought the revolver. Whatever happened in court would not affect her now. If they sentenced her to jail, she had a way out. Meanwhile she continued going to law school. She no longer needed to drink. She no longer felt afraid. She was able to sleep well at night, all except for the night before the early morning when she was to go to court.

When she found that she could not sleep, she got up and made herself some hot chocolate and sat in the big chair beside the window. Her mind, after all the fears and worries of the past few months, was strangely inactive now. She thought of nothing. Not her court appearance, not what might happen, just nothing. She felt a great, comforting calmness envelope her. She sat and watched the fog roll in, listened to the foghorns out on the bay, and smoked and sipped the hot chocolate.

She listened to the traffic sounds in the night. Her only thought was that this would be her last night. The traffic became heavier toward morning, and the parking lot of the International Pancake House across the street began to fill up. The darkness of the night faded. She thought that she was more alive now than she had been the year before in Spokane. Now she could enjoy certain things, the taste of hot chocolate, taking long baths, smoking, the feel of clean pajamas, when, during that awful winter in Spokane, she had been empty, one of the walking dead. Things had got better somehow without her really noticing.

Cecelia held her left hand out in front of her and looked at it the way it looked at that very moment, still wearing the wedding ring. Then she twisted the little gold band. It had been there on that finger for a long time, nearly a decade, and it was only with great difficulty that she finally worked it off.

Her finger felt strange without it, and the circle of skin that the ring covered was very pale. It reminded her of the way a patch of grass in a green lawn looked when it had been covered from the sunlight for a long time and then was uncovered.

She held the gold ring in one hand while she opened the window. The ring was small and light, and even in the dim morning light it gleamed shiny and golden. She made a move as if to toss it out the window, but didn't. It had been hers for too long. She put it in the pocket of her robe, closed the window and went to prepare for her court appearance.

She met her lawyer in the hallway of the courthouse. He was smiling broadly.

"The welfare fraud case has been dismissed, Ms. Welles," he told her.

"Dismissed? You mean just like that? Wiped clean, like it never happened?"

"That's right. Like it never happened. No criminal record. They can't even sue you in civil court."

"But why?"

"Because the welfare department didn't press charges for two years. The statute of limitations."

"Oh, the statute of limitations. Why didn't I think of that?"

The lawyer shrugged, and the two of them went into the courtroom together.

The judge heard her case first. He sentenced her to two days in jail and gave her credit for the time served. He fined her five hundred dollars and ordered her to pay it in five monthly installments and to attend four Monday night classes on safe driving. Then it was all over, and she was free to go. She was stunned.

SEVENTEEN

Cecelia hadn't planned on going to law school that day. She had planned on ending her life after the judge sentenced her. Now she didn't know what to do. It was all mixed up again. The anxiety was back, worse than it had been in a long time. She had thought that it was going to be settled, that there would be no more bad times to deal with ever again. It was being sentenced to jail that she had felt she couldn't bear, and being barred from practicing law because of a crime of moral turpitude. But there would be no more jail. There was no crime. What was she going to do now? How was she going to handle being free? There was too much to do. She wasn't going to be able to lay her burdens down yet. What about Corey and what about Nicole and the divorce. And then being alone and having to make a life for herself and for them. It was too much.

She went to a bar and ordered a glass of white wine. It tasted sour. Her stomach didn't like it, either. She didn't finish it. She thought of her mother and father and what her life had been like when she was a girl. She thought of Bud and how she had loved him and he had been killed. She thought of her welfare-mother years and her marriage that was now over. Her whole life had been painful, she thought, and those days in jail were maybe the most painful of all. She wanted out. She didn't want any more of it.

She tried to push those thoughts away. Weird, destructive thoughts. She wouldn't allow herself to think them, yet they kept crowding back. But she didn't feel like drinking. She decided she had to get rid of that silly, conservative beige court costume she was wearing and those sensible, stuffy, brown leather pumps.

She went into a little antique clothing boutique on Telegraph Avenue and bought herself a beautiful dress from the 1940s. It was navy blue with white polka dots and had shoulder pads. She was pleased with her reflection in the mirror. She would have looked like one of the Andrews Sisters, if only she had had the right kind of hairdo. But her shoes didn't match the dress, and she couldn't find any in the store in her size.

She went down to College Avenue and saw a pair that looked almost like old-style wedgies, only they weren't. Imitation, but still better than her pumps. These shoes were imported from France. It didn't seem right, somehow, but the shoes and dress did seem to go together. She walked out into the street carrying paper bags containing her beige suit and brown pumps and threw them into the nearest litter container. Now what? She thought of going ahead with her plan. That was probably what she should do. If she didn't die, then what would she do? It would just be more of the same.

She couldn't hide out anymore, she thought. She couldn't go on hiding and drinking and going to bed with strange men. She had to struggle this time to push those thoughts away. Stop. Leave me alone. And they did, and her mind was free again.

Cecelia felt giddy, almost euphoric, as she walked around Berkeley, went down University Avenue toward San Pablo, headed for El Cerrito. Her purse was noticeably heavier because of the gun. She wondered why they hadn't checked her for weapons in court. Because traffic offenders don't generally bring firearms to court, probably.

She bought herself a forties-style hairnet and a tube of bright red lipstick. She made up her lips and smiled at her reflection in the little counter mirror. She felt like an actual forties woman who had somehow moved ahead forty years in time.

195

The war was going on. All the men were gone. Maybe she worked in a defense plant and wrote letters to her sweetheart, who was a flying ace. *Bombs Over Tokyo.* What was that song that went, "Hey ya Mister Whatchacallit, Whatcha Doin' Tonight?" —"Muskrat Ramble"? "In the Mood"? Maybe she and some girls from the plant would go to a dance and dance to that kind of music with brave young soldiers. Only she wasn't a young girl. She was thirty years old and that wasn't young, even for 1980. It would probably have been thoroughly middle-aged for the forties. Her husband, then, was the flying ace. He was overseas, of course. She had a framed photograph of him in his uniform. She kept it on the table beside her bed and she kissed it tenderly each night before turning off her light and going to sleep.

Somehow she found herself in the gun shop across from McFarlane's Candy and Ice-Cream Store. When she bought the gun the man had showed her how to load it. Now she purchased a little package of bullets. She would need only one. The man who sold her the bullets said to her, "Thank you and have a nice day," and she said, "You too."

Her spirits were high as she walked out into the bright sunshiny day. Everyone was smiling at everyone else. She was aware of carrying the gun and the bullets.

She saw some blind people with their dark glasses and canes, waiting for the light to change. There were always blind people around El Cerrito Plaza, learning how to get around. That was because the school for the blind was nearby. She remembered reading once that people who were blind from birth, or from a very young age, so young they could not remember ever having had sight, were comfortable in their blindness. If somehow their eyesight was restored, the world became a frightening, confusing place. They knew the way "round" and "square" felt, but not how they looked. They could not perceive depth or spatial relationships with their vision. Sometimes they would retreat back into blindness, going around with dark glasses and canes and their eyes closed just as if they were blind, and then the world became familiar to them again.

She thought what a beautiful day it was. She wished that she

196

had gotten herself an ice-cream cone, a double decker tutti-frutti/rocky road.

The rain had finally stopped. She remembered that Corey and one of his friends had changed the words to a popular song. "I can see clearly now, your head is gone," they would sing, "it's gonna be a bright, bright sunshiny day."

Corey. Nicole. She hadn't meant to think about them.

Cecelia found a phone booth on San Pablo Avenue, dropped a quarter into the slot and dialed the Donahues' number in El Sobrante. She hadn't spoken to them in so long, yet she still knew their number by heart. Bud's father answered the phone. He was surprised to hear her voice.

"I want you to tell me, Frank, about Bud. You never did. No one ever did. How was he killed and where exactly is he buried?" She hadn't wanted to know before. That would have made his death too real.

"He was in a helicopter, Cecelia. The helicopter was shot down. Why do you want to know that?"

"I just wanted to know. Thank you for telling me. Now, please, where is he buried?"

"He's in that big cemetery in El Cerrito on the slope, you must know the one I'm talking about, going up toward Grizzly Peak."

"Yes, I do know, thank you. And one more thing . . ."

"Yes?"

"If anything happens to me, if I die, will you and Mrs. Donahue take Corey? I don't think Nathan is the right person to raise him."

"Yes, of course. You know we would. We would be happy to."

"And would you make sure that Corey and Nicole see each other while they're growing up? They love each other, you know, and they are brother and sister. I think they need to stay in touch."

"Yes. Are you all right, Cecelia?"

"Yes. I'm fine, thank you," she said and hung up the phone.

Cecelia took a taxi to the cemetery. The day had become slightly overcast now. She wished that she had worn a sweater.

She looked among all the tombstones. It was a huge cemetery.

Countless graves. She would never find him on her own. A grounds keeper finally came and asked if he could help. He looked up Bud's name in a directory and showed her to the grave.

"Your brother?" he asked.

"No. He was my husband."

On the little metal marker was Bud's name: Brian Donahue, January 8, 1947–November 3, 1966.

"You don't look old enough," the grounds keeper said, "to have been married in 1966."

"I wasn't," she answered.

The grounds keeper went away and left her at the grave. She tried hard to imagine Bud the way she had known him. She recalled the image of his young face in the photograph the Donahues had given her and she remembered very well how intensely she had loved Bud.

This was not how she would have imagined it. He should have had a gravestone and she would sit there on the grass and talk to the air as if she were talking to him. Her soliloquy might begin, "Well, Bud, it's been a long time. As you can see, I'm not sixteen any more. You and I have a son . . ." the way they did in movies. She would either get it all worked out or she would tell him that she was going to join him now. In movies, though, they don't often join their beloved departed. They usually have the courage to go on.

The grass was wet. Her new, open-toed forties-style shoes were all caked with mud. The cemetery was creepy. It was full of eucalyptus trees. They were not native to the North American continent, were they? Where were they from? Australia? Why didn't they go back to where they came from? Why didn't everyone do that? She had never liked eucalyptus trees, neither their appearance, nor the smell of them, which some people found so fragrant. She didn't like family vaults, either. Vampires always seemed fond of family vaults.

Cecelia sat on the grass getting her new secondhand dress all wet and grass-stained. What did it matter if her dress got stained? She thought of a woman she had once met at an underground BART tunnel waiting for a train. The woman told her she had once tried to jump from the Golden Gate Bridge. She was carrying a suitcase. Someone had come along, some guy from the bridge authority, and talked her down. Inside the suitcase were wigs and negligees. Crazy woman. What silliness, to hold a suitcase full of wigs and negligees as one plunged to one's death.

Cecelia hugged her knees and looked out to the Bay Area, which stretched below her: San Francisco Bay. San Francisco. Alcatraz. She remembered going to Alcatraz during the Indian occupation of 1969. Good feelings out there then. Indians feeling effective. Even skid-row bums had gone to Alcatraz and felt as if they were a part of the Indian people. She remembered the old man in the bar in the Mission District telling her, "We are the biggest tribe of all, us displaced ones, us urban Indians, us sidewalk redskins." He was right.

Cecelia took the gun from her purse and opened the package of bullets. She pushed out the chamber and inserted two bullets. She didn't know why two when one would be enough. She felt tears sting her eyes. She was crying for herself.

She wanted a gravestone. She wanted to be remembered. She wanted someone to visit her grave now and then. And she didn't want to be buried in El Cerrito. She wanted to be buried in northern Idaho in the little tribal cemetery near her dad and her two dead brothers and all the other Captures. Because that was what she was. Cecelia Capture. Cecelia Eagle Capture. But they wouldn't permit the body of a person who had taken her own life to be buried in the tribal cemetery. She had made no provisions for the disposal of her remains. That was stupid. She might end up in a pauper's unmarked grave. But what did it matter to her, after all, what they did with her body when she was gone? She had come this far. She held the revolver in her right hand. Her palm was sweaty.

She thought a moment about Nathan. She had thought that by marrying him she could take on his upbringing, his happy childhood, his confidence, as easily as she had taken on his name. But she couldn't. If she had been able to throw away the grubby little life that she had had, full of worry and struggle, then she would probably be more like Nathan's sisters, one married to a diplomat, the other practicing law in the District Attorney's office and probably grooming herself for a career in politics, which would easily be hers, with the family's connections and money.

But she wasn't like Nathan. She had been the daughter of a half-insane, mean old woman and an ineffective alcoholic father, and she had grown up poor and unwanted. She had been an unmarried welfare mother and had finally become a drunk herself.

She looked at the gun. Shifted it to the other hand. She was stalling. She wondered if Bud was in one piece, not like some guys she had heard stories about, blown to smithereens, the parts of their bodies scattered far and wide, gathered and packed in plastic bags. Bits and pieces. Nineteen years old. If he could somehow come back to life, he would still be nineteen.

She was crying hard now and she had no Kleenexes with her. She wiped her eyes and blew her nose on the hem of her forties dress. Claudette Colbert and Joan Crawford probably never did anything so gauche as to use the hems of their forties dresses to wipe their noses.

She knew that she was not going to kill herself. She was incapable of such a violent act as that. She could not allow her brains and blood to go spattering all over the grass. How would she look? Her face would probably be blown away as well. The whole idea was ridiculous. She was deliberately trying to scare herself, like a kid on a roller coaster or at a scary movie.

But if she did not die, what would she do? Live, of course, and that would take some doing. She wasn't crying any more. She reached down and touched the little metal plaque that marked poor Bud's grave. She was glad that he had left a bit of himself behind in Corey.

She got to her feet. She had been sitting on the cold, wet grass with her legs folded under her for a long while and now her legs ached and felt stiff. She stood still and moved her toes, waited for circulation to return.

The back of her new-old polka-dotted dress was all wet. The cemetery was a long way from a public telephone. She had quite a long walk ahead of her in those silly imported-from-France shoes she had bought.

She removed the bullets from the gun and dropped them on the ground beside Bud's grave. She clicked the chamber back into place and put the gun into her purse. She would throw it away when she found a suitable overgrown spot.

As she made her way down the hill it began to drizzle. She was aware of feeling more lighthearted at this moment, more like herself, than she had felt in a long time.

She had a lot to do now, she thought, now that she was going to live—besides just staying alive—and she wasn't sure how she should approach all her tasks or in which order she should tackle them. And she had to find a place for the three of them to live and a way to support herself and Corey and Nicole. She had to finish her law degree. The logistics of all of this would take some careful planning. Maybe she would have to go see Nathan one more time. Whatever had to be done, she knew she could do it. They were her children and she would have them with her again. She knew this as surely as she knew that she would have the Doctor of Jurisprudence degree.

The drizzle turned into downpour. She would soon be soaked to the skin, but she didn't care. Her long-dead marriage was really over, and knowing this gave her a great feeling of relief. No longer constrained. Not hemmed in. She was not able to return to the beginning, of course, and remake her life more to her liking, but now she was free to go on with the life she did have.

When she reached the iron gate, she looked back just once. It was hard for her to tell where Bud's grave was. She couldn't even see the metal bullets she had dropped. She would be leaving him behind now, too.

"Good-bye, Bud," she whispered, and left the cemetery.